From the Nancy Drew Files

THE CASE: Investigate the strange death of Victory Airlines trainee Rod Fullerton.

CONTACT: Jennifer Bishop, *Nancy's old school friend, now a flight attendant with Victory.*

SUSPECTS: Sean Richmond, *Jennifer's handsome boyfriend. He obviously resents Nancy's investigating.*

Grant Sweeney, *the surly baggage chief who warns Nancy to stay out of his department—or else!*

Miranda Cummings, *the pretty flight attendant who was given a mysterious—and very valuable—Chinese vase by the late Rod Fullerton.*

COMPLICATIONS: It seems almost everybody wants Nancy off this case. Especially the unknown killer who plants a bomb on her flight!

D0756191

Other Nancy Drew Files™ available in Armada

THE NANCY DREW FILES™

Case 13

Wings of Fear

Carolyn Keene

ARMADA

Chapter

One

Br-r-r-ing!

The soft purr of Nancy Drew's bedside phone made her groan in her sleep. She opened one eye, saw that it was after midnight, and promptly covered her head with her pillow.

Br-r-r-ing. Br-r-r-ing.

Groping with one hand, Nancy grabbed the receiver. "Hello?" she said from under the pillow.

"Nancy! Is that you?" The voice on the other end was filled with terror. "You've got to help. Right away! A friend of mine is dead, and I think—I think somebody killed him!"

Nancy blinked in the darkness. "Jennifer? Is

1

that you?" she asked, barely recognizing the voice of her longtime friend, Jennifer Bishop.

"Oh, Nancy, you've got to come! I don't know what to do. Rod was working with me at Victory and then—and then—" She was fighting back sobs. "And then they killed him! I know they did!"

Wide awake by then, Nancy reached over to switch on the bedside lamp. "Wait a minute, Jennifer. Back up. You mean this Rod worked at Victory Airlines with you?"

"Yes, yes. Nancy, you've got to come to Seattle right away and get this straightened out. I'm afraid of who'll be next!"

Jennifer Bishop had once lived near Nancy in River Heights, and she and Nancy had been close friends. After high school graduation, Jennifer had gotten a job as a flight attendant for Victory Airlines, a company based in Seattle, Washington.

Jen didn't usually exaggerate, so Nancy took her at her word. "What makes you so certain Rod was murdered, Jen?"

"I just *know!* He was killed in an automobile accident. His car went wide on a turn and plunged over a cliff. But I know there's more to it than that."

"How do you know?" Nancy pushed strands of reddish blond hair out of her eyes. Murder? Could it really be true?

"He once said that there were people at the airline who knew how to make money. Then he

2

showed me a wad of bills that would have made your eyes pop out! When I asked him how he'd gotten so much cash, he shut up. I kept asking him, and he finally said, kind of jokingly, 'Maybe I'm into smuggling—'" Jennifer inhaled shakily. "But now Rod Fullerton's dead. And I think he was telling the truth!"

Nancy felt a chill go down her spine. "When did he have his car accident?"

"Yesterday."

"And how long ago did he show you the extra cash?"

"He showed me and Miranda the money just last week." Jennifer sounded as if she were gaining control of herself again.

"Who's Miranda?"

"My new roommate. Oh, Nancy, you've just got to come!"

Nancy's mind was spinning ahead. There was nothing keeping her in River Heights. And her close friend, Bess Marvin, had complained of being bored too.

"I'll be there as soon as I can," Nancy said decisively. "And I'll try to bring Bess. You remember Bess Marvin, don't you?"

"Oh, Nan, I knew I could count on you. Just hurry, please."

Nancy could barely sleep the rest of the night. By the time her father joined her for breakfast, she had already checked into flights to Seattle and packed her bags.

"What's up?" Carson Drew asked as he sat down in the chair across from Nancy's.

"I've got a chance to go to Seattle and visit my friend Jennifer Bishop," Nancy said, glancing at the clock on the kitchen wall.

"Planning to go right this minute?" Carson asked, smiling.

"I wish I could," Nancy said and filled him in on Jennifer's call.

Her father's expression grew grave as she mentioned Jennifer's suspicions about Rod Fullerton.

"I have only one piece of advice," he said. "The same advice I give you every time you get involved in a mystery: be careful."

Nancy kissed his cheek. "I promise, Dad. I've got to go now—I have to talk to Bess."

Bess peered out cautiously before throwing the door open for her friend. "What are you doing up so early?" she asked in surprise. "Wait—don't answer that. Another case, right?"

Bess was still in her robe, and she motioned for Nancy to follow her to her bedroom. "So what's this all about?" she asked.

"I don't know for sure yet. Maybe smuggling. And murder."

Nancy found a relatively clean place to sit on the end of Bess's bed. Clothes were strewn all over—which was typical for her friend.

"I couldn't decide what to wear," Bess explained defensively as she noticed Nancy looking

4

at the mess in her room. She snatched up a pair of black jeans from the floor and pulled them on. "Now, tell all."

Nancy nodded soberly. "You remember Jennifer Bishop, don't you?"

"Didn't she go to work for an airline?"

"Victory Airlines," Nancy said and quickly filled Bess in on Jennifer's phone call. Nancy concluded by saying, "I want you to come with me."

Bess almost dropped her comb. "Really? I'd love to! I love the West Coast!"

"So you're with me?"

"All the way!"

It didn't take long to finalize the details of their trip. Nancy made their airline reservations. Then they said goodbye to Bess's cousin, George Fayne, who was sorry to see them leave but too busy to join them. Finally, Nancy called Jennifer and left a message on her answering machine telling her when they'd be arriving.

"Brrr." Bess shivered as they boarded their Victory plane in Chicago. "I hope it's warmer in Seattle."

"The paper said it would be clear and cool," Nancy said, glancing around as they boarded flight 304. The flight attendant—her scarlet blouse a dramatic contrast to her black and gold Victory uniform—showed them their seats. After Jennifer's phone call, Nancy half expected to see something unusual on the plane, but the flight was uneventful. In a few hours they were circling above Puget Sound Airport.

"I've always envied Jennifer her job," Nancy said as she looked out over Seattle. Puget Sound glimmered in the afternoon sun. In the distance Nancy could see a ferry chugging from Seattle's waterfront to an island in the sound.

"Me, too." Bess sighed. "Think of all the fantastic places she gets to see."

"Like the Far East," Nancy said. "Victory mainly serves the West Coast and the Orient. They have only a few flights to Chicago, New York, and Dallas."

"The Orient." Bess closed her eyes, smiling wistfully. "Hong Kong, Tokyo, the Philippines . . ."

"You'll have to settle for Seattle today," Nancy said, her eyes sparkling. "Oh, it's gorgeous. Look, there's Mount Rainier."

After the girls had deplaned and collected their bags from the baggage carousel, they looked around for Jennifer.

"Do you think she got the message about our flight?" Bess asked, shifting her shoulder bag.

"I hope so," Nancy answered. "Hey, how much stuff did you bring? It looks as if you packed for a year!"

Bess was surrounded by all kinds of canvas luggage. "I wanted to be prepared," she said defensively. "You never know what you might need."

Nancy laughed. Unlike Bess, she always packed light. In fact, every once in a while she wished she had remembered to bring one more outfit. "Well, these'll have to do me," she said, glancing down at her black-and-white plaid pants and bulky magenta cardigan. "If I need to dress up I'm going to have a big problem. Let's go get our rental car. Maybe Jennifer will show up by the time we're done."

After she had collected the car keys and really begun to worry that Jennifer hadn't gotten the message, a petite, pretty girl came toward them. Arms waving, her curly dark hair a wild cloud around her head, Jennifer weaved among the milling passengers.

"Nancy! Bess!" she shouted. "Sorry I'm late. I was talking to Preston Talbot and I forgot the time."

Nancy grinned at her friend. "Forgotten for a boy. I should have known it!"

Jennifer laughed. "Preston Talbot is no boy. He's the president of Victory Airlines, and he wants to see you immediately! When I realized how big this thing might be, I went straight to the top. He was really anxious to hear what I had to say."

With a sinking feeling Nancy realized her trip to Seattle was no longer a secret. But how much had Jennifer told?

"Here, let me take that," Jennifer said, grabbing one of Bess's bags and walking quickly toward the escalators. "We've got to hurry. I told Mr. Talbot I'd find you and come straight back to his office."

Nancy and Bess had no choice but to follow after her, lugging all of Bess's bags. They continued to talk as they walked toward the Victory flight counter.

"I'm glad I told Mr. Talbot. I just can't get Rod's death off my mind."

Nancy was going to reserve judgment on Mr. Talbot until after she had met him. "Did Rod have a lot of friends at Victory?" she asked.

"Some. Miranda, my roommate, would know. She knew him better than I did."

"Does Victory have this entire section?" Bess asked, staring at the busy flight counter as they passed.

"Uh-huh. We started out small, but we've just expanded," Jennifer said proudly. "Now we fly daily to Tokyo and Taipei, and we have service to other major cities two and three times a week."

"Have you ever worked on a flight to the Far East?" Bess asked.

"Sure. But right now I'm doing the flight to Los Angeles and back." She took them to a door to the right of Victory's counter and added, "This leads to all of Victory's inner offices. We rent space from the airport."

"How long had Rod worked here?" Nancy asked, getting back to the main topic.

"About a year, I guess. Maybe two. It just seems so unbelievable that he's gone." Jennifer's face darkened. "Rod was a skycap. He was part of Victory's management trainee program."

"Management trainee program?" Nancy repeated.

"We have a work-study program done in cooperation with one of the colleges here," Jennifer explained. "The students involved start out doing everything: baggage handling, being skycaps and gate agents. They even take a crash course in being flight attendants."

"Are these students girls or guys?" Bess asked, her eyes brightening with interest.

"Both. My boyfriend, Sean, is in the program. Right now there're more guys than girls."

Bess smiled. "This is sounding better and better," she murmured.

For the first time Jennifer grinned. "Sean can introduce you to some of the guys he knows. He's been working as a baggage handler, but in a couple of weeks, he's going to be a gate agent."

Down a gray-carpeted hallway the girls caught one of three private elevators that led up to Victory's seven floors of offices. Jennifer punched the button for the sixth floor, and the elevator whizzed silently upward. At the sixth floor a bell dinged softly as the doors whispered open.

"Mr. Talbot is a really busy man," Jennifer said as she led them to an impressive set of oak double doors. "But after I told him about the smuggling ring he said I could stop by anytime until we get this thing cleared up."

"We don't know that there is any smuggling for sure," Nancy reminded her quickly.

"Well, I thought Rod's remark made that pretty clear," Jennifer answered. "And Mr. Talbot was really concerned when I told him. I also let him know that I'd be with you, helping all the way."

Nancy was beginning to realize that Jennifer wanted to be very involved in the investigation. She had begged Nancy to come help, yet she seemed determined to take the investigation out of Nancy's hands before Nancy had had a chance to do anything!

Raising her hand to knock, Jennifer said, "I'll just tell Mr. Talbot that you're here—"

Jennifer never completed her thought. From inside the room came a loud, shattering crash and the sound of breaking glass. It sounded as if someone, or something, had smashed through a window!

Chapter

Two

JENNIFER, NANCY, AND BESS raced into Mr. Talbot's office. Preston Talbot was staring at a hole in his window, shards of glass still falling to the floor.

"What happened?" Nancy demanded. Then she heard footsteps pounding against metal outside. She ran to the broken window. A heavy metal catwalk surrounded the building on the sixth floor. She thought she saw a hooded figure round the far corner. "Where does this walkway go?" she asked.

Mr. Talbot waved vaguely in the same direction the figure had gone. "The north side."

Nancy turned away from the window. She knew

11

there was no way she'd be able to reach her quarry in time.

Jennifer interrupted her thoughts, saying, "These are the friends I was telling you about—Bess Marvin and Nancy Drew."

Still looking slightly dazed, Preston Talbot came from behind his desk to shake Nancy's and Bess's hands. "Jennifer told me you were coming."

Nancy would have picked Preston Talbot as the kind of man to run an airline. He had thinning gray hair, an immaculate suit, and a face that seemed lined in perpetual worry. "What was thrown through the window?" she asked him.

"I don't know. I was just sitting here. All of a sudden . . ." He trailed off, frowning. "It was a rock, I think. It rolled under that chair."

"You're lucky it didn't hit you," Bess remarked as Nancy bent to pick up the rock.

"It's got a note wrapped around it!" Jennifer exclaimed as Nancy brought it out. She looked over Nancy's shoulder eagerly as Nancy undid the rubber bands holding the note to the rock.

A message had been pasted together from letters cut out of a magazine: "Nancy Drew, if you value your life, leave Seattle *now!*"

Jennifer gasped and Bess made a choking sound. Nancy looked at her two friends. "Someone else knows I'm here," she said uneasily.

"Let me see that." Preston Talbot practically snatched the note from her hands. "I'm beginning to think you're right about something going on at Victory, Jennifer," he said.

Glancing at Nancy, he added, "Frankly, Ms. Drew, before this happened, I thought calling you in was a mistake. Victory has an excellent reputation, and I didn't want any amateur detective coming around to stir up trouble."

"Oh, Nancy's no amateur," Bess put in loyally. "She's solved all kinds of mysteries. Some really dangerous ones."

"Even so, I didn't want anyone poking around. Now I'm not so sure—"

"Since I'm already here, maybe I can help," Nancy said briskly. She bent to examine the note. "Whoever wrote this means business. Someone obviously knew I was coming to your office. Did you see the person who threw the rock?"

"No. I was just reaching for the phone when this thing smashed through the window. I ran to look but the figure I saw just flashed by."

"A hooded figure?"

Talbot looked at Nancy in surprise. "Why, yes! I think he had on one of the black slickers the baggage handlers wear in bad weather."

"But it's sunny today," Nancy said, glancing out of the window.

Beyond the catwalk several of Victory's docking gates could be seen. A Victory plane, the gold *V* on its tail winking in the sun, stood ready for loading. Talbot's office had an excellent view of Victory's entire operation.

"Do you think we should go to the police?" Bess asked nervously. "That note's a threat, Nancy!"

"I'd rather we didn't call the police yet," Mr. Talbot interjected quickly. "I've got an airline to think of. I don't want its image tainted by smuggling unless it's true."

"Rod only hinted that smuggling was involved," Nancy pointed out. She was feeling more and more annoyed with Jennifer for having jumped the gun. "We don't know for sure. I can do some investigating to find out what's really going on if you'd like, Mr. Talbot."

"Great idea." Mr. Talbot sounded immensely relieved. "Go ahead and ask all the questions you want. I'll get you a pass that'll allow you to go anywhere on the premises. It'll certainly be better than having the police involved," he muttered. He seemed to be talking to himself as much as to the girls.

Nancy was anxious to get started then before Mr. Talbot changed his mind. "I'd like to talk to the baggage handlers. If smuggling is involved, they'd be the ones who would load the cargo."

"And that slicker was like the ones the handlers wear," Jennifer reminded her.

"That's right."

"What do you want me to do?" Bess asked.

Mr. Talbot looked at her and smiled for the first time. "How would you like to be a temporary flight attendant?" he suggested. "There's a two-

14

day crash FAA course starting tomorrow. Jennifer can fill you in on the rest of the basics, and you could be in the air by Friday!"

"Oh, wow," Bess said excitedly.

"But *I'll* be up in the air," Jennifer protested. "I can handle that end of it."

"Sometimes it's nice to have a friend with you when it gets dangerous," Nancy said, trying to tread softly. She didn't want to alienate her friend, but she was worried that Jennifer thought she could handle it all. "Besides, Bess has always dreamed of flying."

"Then it's settled," Mr. Talbot said, shaking Nancy's hand again. "Good luck. And I hope you can put these smuggling rumors to rest."

"I'm glad you get to fly," Jennifer said to Bess as they left the office. "But I could have handled that part on my own."

"Don't worry," Nancy put in quickly. "We're all in this together."

Jennifer's green eyes flashed. "Great! I've always wanted to do what you do. Detective work is so exciting!"

Nancy gave a short laugh. "I guess it's a case of the grass being greener on the other side. I sort of wish I could be a flight attendant," she said over her shoulder as she ran to the end of the hall for a minute.

"Really? Well, then, maybe you and Bess should trade places," Jennifer said, raising her voice.

"Oh, no." Bess shook her blond head emphatically. "I'll leave the crime solving to Nancy any day. Just let me up on that plane. How old are the pilots, anyway?"

"It depends." Jennifer's eyes twinkled. "There's a cute copilot who flies the L.A. flight. I'll introduce you."

"What are we waiting for?" Bess started walking faster.

When they got to the elevator, Nancy rejoined them. "Who has access to those locked doors at the end of the hall?" she asked.

"Mr. Talbot, I suppose. I don't know. I think they're conference rooms."

"Can you get to that catwalk through those doors?"

Jennifer shook her head. "No. The catwalk ends at the outdoor stairway. It's like an emergency exit for the upper floors."

"So the person who threw the rock probably climbed up from the ground or down from the roof," Nancy said thoughtfully.

Jennifer nodded. "Whoever it was knows his way around the building," she added.

Jennifer had ridden to the airport that day with Sean, so all three girls climbed into Nancy's rental car. Jennifer pointed the way toward her apartment. Soon they were heading down the freeways that surrounded Seattle's city center.

On the way, Nancy had time to think. Who'd thrown the rock? Someone had to be monitoring her moves pretty closely to know she'd been about to enter Mr. Talbot's office. Or maybe they had only known she was coming to Seattle and had tossed the rock in, figuring the president would find out who she was and what she was doing.

But how had the word gotten out that she was coming?

"Did you tell anyone else about me besides Mr. Talbot?" Nancy asked Jennifer.

"Just Miranda and Sean. They're both at my apartment, waiting to meet you."

Jennifer's apartment turned out to be close to the freeway and therefore to the airport. "Sometimes we change assignments at a moment's notice," she explained. "And if we miss a flight . . ." She drew her finger across her throat. "It's curtains."

"But if you were late because of an emergency, wouldn't they have to understand?" Bess asked as Nancy parked the car.

"You haven't met Linda Cotilla yet," Jennifer said ominously. "She's one of our senior flight attendants. You could have triple pneumonia, a flat tire, and amnesia all at the same time—and she still wouldn't understand."

"Will I have to fly with her?" Bess asked anxiously as Jennifer opened the door to her apartment.

"Probably."

"Great. Just what I need. Trouble." Bess sighed.

"Who's in trouble?" a male voice asked.

Turning, Nancy saw a young man with dark hair and devilish blue eyes at the door. He was wearing a black leather flight jacket stamped with the distinctive gold *V* for Victory.

"Sean," Jennifer said, slipping her arm through his, "these are my friends Nancy Drew and Bess Marvin. My boyfriend, Sean Richmond."

"So you're the detective!" Sean said to Nancy. "Jen's told me a lot about you."

Sean was one of the handsomest guys Nancy had seen in a long time. She darted a quick glance at Bess, who was looking totally starstruck.

"Hey, what about me?" another voice interrupted before Nancy could respond. A pretty redhead poked her head around the corner. She was dressed in a Victory uniform just like Jennifer's. "I'm Jennifer's roommate, Miranda Cummings," she said with a friendly smile.

"Come on in the kitchen," Jennifer invited, "and grab some potato chips. I thought we'd just have hamburgers for dinner."

"Great!" Bess said enthusiastically. "I'll start my diet tomorrow."

That was such a pat phrase in her friend's vocabulary that Nancy had to swallow a smile.

"Who's in trouble?" Sean asked again as they all crowded around the tiny kitchen table.

"I am," Bess said, sighing. "I'm sure I'll be all thumbs my first few days as a flight attendant."

18

"Bess is starting FAA training tomorrow," Jennifer explained to Sean and Miranda. "She'll be flying with me. I was just warning her about Linda Cotilla."

"Cotilla the Hun?" Miranda said with a mock shudder. "Flying with that woman is murder. I should know—I just got off a flight with her."

"She was bad, huh?" Jennifer looked sympathetic.

"I don't know what's the matter with her. She just gets worse and worse. She snaps out orders, forgets what she's said, and then gets mad when we do something she's just asked us to. The woman is totally stressed out."

Nancy was startled. That was odd behavior for someone who was supposed to keep a cool head during crises. "Did Linda know Rod Fullerton?" she asked.

Miranda just stared at her. "No," she said tersely. "Linda wasn't the kind of person to associate with Rod."

Oops! Nancy thought. Jennifer had mentioned that Miranda knew Rod well. "I'm sorry," Nancy said. "Rod was a friend of yours."

Miranda's lips tightened, and for a moment Nancy was afraid she might cry. But instead she just helped Jennifer with the hamburgers and said nothing.

"I can show you around the airport tomorrow and introduce you to a few people," Sean suggested to Nancy. "If you're willing to get up early, I can pick you up on my way to work."

"That's no problem for Nancy. She gets up with the sparrows," Bess complained.

"You will be, too." Jennifer grinned. "Starting tomorrow."

Bess groaned dramatically.

"Since I'm probably going to be at the airport all day, I'd love a ride," Nancy answered Sean. "Then Bess can have the rental car if she needs it." Nancy was glad when Jennifer told her she'd be working the flight to L.A. and therefore out of her hair for a while. Nancy needed time to work on the investigation without anyone's meddling—well-meant or otherwise.

Jennifer and Miranda declined Nancy and Bess's offer to help with dinner, so the girls went out to the car and brought in their luggage. They'd decided to accept Jennifer's invitation and camp out in her living room rather than stay in a hotel.

They all crowded around the kitchen table and ate the hamburgers off paper plates. Nancy would have liked to catch up on what was happening in Jennifer's life, but Jen turned the conversation to Rod's mysterious death time and time again. And she kept mentioning the smuggling angle.

She's really getting into this, Nancy thought, worried.

Miranda grew quieter and quieter. Suddenly she jumped up and ran out of the room.

"Hey, what's the matter?" Jennifer asked.

Then Miranda rushed back in with a beautiful vase in her hand. Thrusting it at Nancy, she exclaimed, "Here, you take this! I don't want it! I didn't steal it! It was a present! I'm *not* a smuggler!"

Chapter

Three

T HIS WAS STOLEN?" Nancy asked, amazed.

"I don't know." Miranda looked frightened. "Rod gave it to me. We dated for a while last year. He gave me the vase as a gift. But if it's stolen, I don't want it!"

Jennifer stared raptly at the vase. "Rod must have smuggled it in!" she said breathily.

"We don't know anything for sure," Nancy said sharply. She turned the lovely piece over in her hands. It was a deep, rich blue color with a scene of flowers, a bridge, and a stream overlaid with a lustrous gold-filigreed paint.

"Is it valuable?" Jennifer asked eagerly.

23

Nancy frowned. "It looks really old, but maybe it's made to look that way."

"I don't care whether it's valuable or not!" Miranda declared. "I don't want it!"

Nancy had taken a course in art appreciation, and just the year before the Art Institute in Chicago had had an exhibit of Chinese art. She had seen similar Chinese vases from the Ming Dynasty. But she wasn't able to distinguish an original from a fake.

"If this *is* real, it's worth a fortune," Nancy said.

"Well, then it must be fake," Sean said. "I don't care how much cash Rod was tossing around, he didn't have *that* much money."

Nancy's brows lifted. "Unless he wasn't kidding about the smuggling," she said thoughtfully.

Jennifer jumped up from her chair. "See?" she said triumphantly. "I was right!"

"Hang on to the vase until we know more. Put it somewhere safe," Nancy said to Miranda. "It might be important later."

Miranda gingerly took the vase from Nancy's hands. "Do you really think it's valuable?"

With a grim smile, Nancy said, *"That's* what I intend to find out. If it is, we've got a pretty good case for smuggling."

The next day Bess began her training. Jennifer took off on her daily Seattle–Los Angeles round trip. Sean picked Nancy up at six-thirty in the morning, and they drove to the airport.

"Were you and Rod friends?" Nancy asked as they walked to the terminal from the parking lot. She pulled her red wool coat more firmly around herself as the wind gusted.

"Sort of. I had a few training classes with him. He was a regular sort of guy. We used to do stuff together, but I never got too close to him. He was kind of secretive."

"Secretive in what way?"

"He just didn't like to talk about himself. I went to his apartment one time. It was pretty bad. If Jen says he flashed money around, I believe her, but he must have gotten it fairly recently."

They entered through the main level and crossed the gray-and-black carpet to the Victory flight counter.

"You were here yesterday, right?" Sean asked.

"We just passed by on our way to Mr. Talbot's office. I didn't really get to meet anyone."

"Well, then, let me introduce you." Sean started introducing Nancy to every Victory employee in sight. There were so many names and faces that Nancy's head began to spin. Sean seemed to know most everyone, but none of them had the time to talk. They were all getting ready for the day.

After Nancy picked up her Victory identification badge, she stood around and waited until some of the employees would have time to answer her questions.

"See the guy who just came through the back door behind the counter? That's Blake Maxell. He's Victory's district manager," Sean said, standing with Nancy still.

"What does he do?"

Sean grinned. "He's got the job I want someday! Which is why I'm in the management trainee program. Maxell is in charge of operations—the day-to-day workings of the airline. Talbot may be the president, but he only deals with the airline's public image, stuff like that. Maxell's got his hands in the actual running of the airline."

Nancy tucked that piece of information away. "Could I meet some of the people who actually load the baggage and go inside the baggage compartment?" she asked. "You know, skycaps, cleaning crew, baggage handlers? If there's smuggling going on, some of them would have to know about it."

"Your wish is my command."

Sean was so friendly and attractive that Nancy could easily see how Jennifer had fallen for him. She thought about her longtime boyfriend, Ned Nickerson, and wished he could have come with her on this trip. But Ned was at school at Emerson College and couldn't get away then.

Still, she missed him. And being with Sean just reminded her of how much she really cared for Ned.

Sean took Nancy downstairs. She felt as if she were descending into a dark catacomb. The hallways were narrow, low-ceilinged, and the walls were gray-painted cinder blocks. After zigzagging down several corridors, Sean opened a door that led into a wide room where a belt delivered baggage into a low-walled receptacle. As they walked in, huge metal doors on the far wall rattled open, and a small tractor-type vehicle pulling several small trailers drove in from the loading area. Instantly the baggage handlers began loading suitcases, bags, and packages into the trailers.

"Hey, Richmond!" somebody yelled. "Nice you could finally make it."

Sean grinned. "Give me a break, okay? I'm only fifteen minutes late, and I had something to do."

A low whistle followed as one of the guys looked Nancy's way. "So I see!"

"That's Paul," Sean said in an aside to Nancy. "A regular cut-up. He's a nice guy, though."

Nancy smiled. All the baggage handlers wore black pants and shirts and leather jackets like Sean's. And all of them looked as if they were dying for introductions.

"Come on, Richmond," Paul said. He ran his hand over his sandy brown hair, his eyes sparkling. "You've already got one girl. Spread the wealth!"

Sean was just about to answer when a man suddenly strode up from the back of the room, glowering at them, his expression as dark as his hair. He didn't waste time with preliminaries. "You know it's against the rules to bring anyone down here," he said angrily to Sean. "Now get her out of here and get back to work! You're late!"

"Mr. Talbot asked Sean to show me around," Nancy quickly inserted, showing him the Victory Airlines identification card.

"Well, you'll have to come back another time," the man said gruffly. "We're busy down here."

He strode away, shooting one last cold glance at Sean.

"Whoops," Sean murmured. "I'd better get to work."

"Who's *he?*" Nancy asked.

"Grant Sweeney. He's the guy in charge of baggage—my boss, so to speak. But he hates dealing with us management trainees. I think he's jealous."

Nancy melted into the background while Sean went to work. She didn't want to cause him any more trouble, but she really needed to have a look around.

There was a load of large rectangular crates at one end of the room. Casually Nancy walked over to check them out. But they were just crates of fruit being shipped from overseas to the U.S. Nancy realized this cargo couldn't have anything to do with the Chinese vase Rod had given Miranda. Was Miranda's vase valuable? she wondered again.

Nancy had just finished examining the last group of crates when Grant Sweeney reappeared behind her.

"What are you looking for?" he asked suspiciously.

"Nothing in particular." She gave him a wide smile. Then she suddenly said, "Actually, I was wondering if there were any Chinese vases in these boxes." She knew that sometimes the only way to gain information was to light a fire under someone.

"Chinese vases?" Sweeney repeated in a voice so quiet and threatening that Nancy was sure she had pushed the right button.

"That's right. I'm really interested in them," she said innocently. "A friend of mine was telling me she bought some—"

"Who sent you down here?" he cut her off. "You don't belong down here. What do you think you're doing?"

"Mr. Sweeney?" one of the baggage handlers called from the other side of the room.

Grant looked over his shoulder, moved in a little closer to Nancy, then suddenly turned on his heel and left. "I want you out of here," he ordered Nancy over his shoulder.

"Yes, *sir*," she said under her breath.

Nancy left the baggage room and went back upstairs. She didn't know whether Sweeney was just normally suspicious or if he was mixed up in something sinister, but she didn't want to hang around and find out. She needed information first. And except for the threatening note—and maybe Miranda's vase—there was nothing to suggest that a smuggling operation existed, that a murder had been committed, or even that Victory Airlines was connected with anything illegal.

Standing in the center of the lobby, Nancy looked around. She couldn't decide what to do next. For lack of anything better, she checked Victory's flight schedule and noticed that flight 222 from Korea was coming in late. At that moment, over the loudspeaker, a voice intoned, "Victory flight thirty-eight to Singapore has been delayed two hours. We are sorry for any inconvenience it may cause you. Please check at the flight desk if you need to change your plans."

A groan sounded loud next to Nancy's ear. "That's because that Korea flight's late," a man grumbled. "After they check it out and clean it up, the same plane takes off for Singapore. Now what'll I do? I've already waited two hours! How much longer will it take?"

Nancy looked around to see a disgruntled-looking man checking his watch. "Do you know why the flight's late out of Korea?" she asked.

"Mechanical difficulty, or so they say." He threw a scathing glance over his shoulder at the Victory flight counter and stomped off in a huff.

Nancy checked her own watch. It wasn't doing her any good to just stand around.

Sean had agreed to meet her for lunch, so she

had a couple of hours free. She used them trying to ask questions. Whenever she talked to someone, she casually brought up Rod Fullerton's name, hoping for some kind of reaction.

But she struck out all around. By noon the only person who'd acted even the least bit strange was Grant Sweeney.

At twelve-ten Sean appeared from the baggage area. "Come on," he said. "Let's grab something to eat and then go down to the gates so you can meet some of the gate agents."

"I haven't been having much luck finding out anything here," Nancy admitted as they headed toward Concourse L, where most of Victory's flights came in.

"Don't worry, your luck's going to change. I can feel it," Sean said encouragingly.

They ate lunch at a small café, and after lunch Sean introduced her to other Victory employees, but she had no more success than before. Either no one knew anything, or no one was talking.

"I can't find one person who seems to have known Rod very well," she said, puzzled. "I wonder why."

"As I said, he was secretive." Sean was walking her back to the front of the terminal. "There was one thing odd about him, though. All of us in the management trainee program are college students. It's a prerequisite. But Rod never went to college—and he was in the program, too."

"How did he get in?"

Sean shrugged. "Beats me."

He went back to work, and Nancy continued asking questions. She thought about what Sean had said. What had Rod's connection to Victory been?

Maybe she'd get more answers from the people who were part of the program. Nancy decided to concentrate on them for a while. But no one appeared to know anything more.

Toward the end of the day Nancy went back to the baggage-handling area. She'd decided it was worth risking a fight with Grant Sweeney to get some answers.

Nancy glanced nervously around. She was glad to see that Sweeney wasn't in sight. Most of the other handlers were eager to talk to her. But all of them were more interested in offering to show her around Seattle than in helping with the case.

"I'm discouraged," she told Sean when she met him after his shift was over. "Nobody even acted the least bit suspicious. Everyone just looked frazzled when I tried to interrupt them."

"Maybe there's just nothing going on here," he suggested. "No mystery. Come on, Jen's flight is probably in already. Let's catch her before she heads home."

He grabbed Nancy's hand and led her toward gate 43. But when they got there, it was to find that Jennifer's flight had already emptied. No one was around except one of the other flight attendants.

"Jennifer?" the flight attendant said reflectively when Sean asked her if she knew where Jennifer had gone. "You know, I think she said she was going to see the president. She was all excited about something."

Nancy didn't like the sound of that. "We'd better find her fast," she said in a low voice to Sean. "Before she gets herself in real danger!"

They hurried toward Victory's inner offices and the elevators that led upstairs. Nancy watched the floors light up one by one. She was relieved when they finally got to the sixth floor—and saw Jennifer in front of Mr. Talbot's door.

"Jennifer!" Sean exclaimed.

Jennifer whipped around, her eyes bright. "Guess what!" she said excitedly. "I've done it. I've cracked the smuggling ring all by myself!"

Chapter

Four

"SAY THAT AGAIN," Nancy said, staring at her friend.

At that moment Preston Talbot opened his door. "Jennifer!" he said, surprised. "Ms. Drew—"

"I've cracked the case, Mr. Talbot!" Jennifer interrupted proudly.

"*You've* cracked the smuggling ring?" Talbot was amazed. "How?"

Nancy was anxious to hear what Jennifer had to say, too.

"It was on the flight from L.A.," Jen began eagerly. "There was a group of men in first class. They all wore dark suits and carried briefcases.

They made it clear they didn't want anyone else around them. But I was suspicious, so I peeked over my shoulder when they opened up one of the briefcases. You know what I saw?" Jennifer drew a deep breath. "Diamonds! Hundreds of them!" She looked from Preston Talbot to Sean to Nancy, waiting for some kind of response.

Nancy hardly knew what to say. "Are you sure they were diamonds?" she asked tentatively. It didn't fit in, somehow, with the leads she had so far.

"Sure, I'm sure!" When no one said anything, Jennifer added, a little defensively, "Well, they *looked* like them. And the men were acting so secretive."

Talbot steepled his fingers on his desk. "They could have been legitimate businessmen," he said. "I'll look into it."

"With loot like that?" Jennifer's face was flushed.

"It might have been costume jewelry," Nancy said. "They could be salesmen. It might even be fairly valuable, so they don't want anyone watching them."

Jennifer's lips parted in disbelief. "You won't listen to anything I have to say, will you?" And she swept out of the room.

Nancy caught her in the hallway. "Relax, Jen. It might be a valuable clue—we just don't know yet. Come on, let's go back inside."

Sean and Preston Talbot were standing in the center of the room. They'd been deep in conversation when Nancy and Jennifer came in, but now they broke apart. Nancy wondered what they'd been discussing so intently.

"I don't really like your being so involved in all this," Sean said to Jennifer. "It worries me."

Jennifer flushed. "I'm a big girl, Sean. I can take care of myself."

Because he was obviously waiting for some kind of explanation, Nancy filled Preston Talbot in on the newest developments of the case. She explained about Miranda's vase and Grant Sweeney's aversion to her "snooping around."

Mr. Talbot seemed particularly alarmed at the vase. "I-I'll have to get an expert to check it out," he said hastily.

A few minutes later Nancy, Jennifer, and Sean left and headed back to the main floor. Jen still seemed irritated. Nancy wished she could tell her friend to quit trying so hard, but Jennifer wasn't listening to her. A dark scowl lined her pretty face, and her chin stuck out determinedly.

"Look, the most important thing is that we work together," Nancy said, trying to hold back her exasperation. "It doesn't get us anywhere if we keep jumping to conclusions."

"You mean if *I* keep jumping to conclusions." Jennifer's eyes flashed.

Sean put his arm around her. "Let's just forget

the whole thing for a while and go get something to eat."

"That's a great idea," Nancy seconded, sounding relieved. "Bess should be back from flight class soon. Why don't we all go get a pizza?"

Sean agreed eagerly. He tried to urge Jennifer toward the door, but her silence was like a time bomb ticking away.

"For pete's sake, let's not fight!" Nancy said impatiently. "We don't get to see each other that often."

"I just want to help," Jennifer said in a hurt tone. "But none of you will listen to me!"

"Okay, Jennifer." Nancy pulled her to one of the scarlet couches grouped opposite the Victory flight counter. "What do you want to do?"

"*I* want to eat," Sean said, "and forget this whole stupid thing for a while."

"Well, I want to be a part of Nancy's detecting team," Jennifer spoke up. "I want to know what's happened. I don't want to be shoved around and not know what's going on."

"How about if we go over everything we've learned so far?" Nancy said diplomatically. "Then we'll set it aside until after dinner. Agreed?"

After a pause, Jennifer grudgingly said, "Agreed."

Sean just shook his head and looked resigned.

"It all started with Rod Fullerton's death," Jennifer said. Nancy could tell she was getting back into her role.

38

"Actually, it started with Fullerton's bankroll and his mysterious comment about being involved with smuggling," Nancy said.

"No." Jennifer shook her head. "It was more than that. I'd had a feeling something was up with Rod for a long time. It was just the way he acted."

"How?" Nancy asked.

"As if he was involved in something," Jennifer said. "Whenever I saw him here at the airport, he acted as if he could hardly keep his secret—whatever it was."

"That's true," Sean admitted. "But Rod was always kind of that way."

"Did he ever hint any more about this smuggling ring?" Nancy asked.

"No, he never mentioned anything," Jennifer said. Then her brow puckered thoughtfully. "Except—"

"What?"

"Well, this is silly, but once in a while he'd say 'seven forty-seven' and then grin as though he'd told a really funny joke."

"Seven forty-seven?" Nancy repeated blankly. "Like the jet?"

Jennifer shrugged. "I guess."

The voice over the loudspeaker broke into their conversation. "Flight thirty-eight for Singapore now ready for boarding."

Sean pricked up his ears. "That flight's finally ready to leave, huh? I guess they must have fixed the mechanical problem if they're sending it out again."

Nancy suddenly grabbed Jennifer's arm. "A seven forty-seven's a jumbo jet, isn't it?"

"Well, yeah. Everybody knows that." Jennifer lifted her brows.

"And this flight to Singapore? The one that came from Korea? It's probably a seven forty-seven."

Before she had finished speaking, Nancy was on her way to the flight desk, Jennifer and Sean at her heels. At the first opportunity Nancy asked what type of airplane was being used for flight 38.

"A seven forty-seven," the agent said.

"I've got to see inside that plane," Nancy said tersely, turning to Sean and Jennifer.

"Now?" they both echoed.

"Maybe there's something still in the baggage compartment. I've got to see before it takes off again."

"But it's been unloaded, and they're ready to load up again," Sean argued.

"Let's go see."

Jennifer sighed impatiently. "I can see you don't need *me*. I'll just stay here and wait. Whenever you decide you're finished, we'll go pick up Bess."

Nancy opened her mouth to argue, but Jennifer was walking back toward the group of chairs they'd just left. Because she didn't have the time to make her friend feel better, Nancy hurried down through the lower level to the baggage room, then out through the metal doors and across the asphalt to the big-bodied jet.

Sean was right behind her. "Slow down!" he yelled.

"I don't have time!" Nancy shouted above the high-pitched whine from a departing plane. The noise outside was deafening.

Sean motioned her around to the side, tried to say something to her, then gave up and pointed to the movable staircase shoved against the side of the plane next to the baggage compartment. "Flight thirty-eight to Singapore," he mouthed. "I'll wait for you."

Nancy's lips parted. The plane was enormous! The tires alone were taller than she was!

She knew she was taking a risk, but she had a hunch that she was on to something. Mounting the stairs, her hair flying wildly in the buffeting wind, Nancy entered the rear of the plane, where the baggage was stored.

There was no one in sight, only boxes and suitcases piled to the ceiling. With a sinking heart, Nancy realized Sean had been right. The plane had already been loaded for Singapore. If anything had been smuggled in, it was already in the terminal's baggage hold or being held at customs. She'd been too hasty in her search for a clue.

Disappointed, Nancy gave one last look around and noticed a group of boxes that had been shoved to one side. She did a double take when she saw the labels. The point of origin seemed to be Korea!

With rising excitement Nancy shoved her way through the luggage to get a closer look. Was there a reason these parcels were still on the plane? Was it a way to avoid customs? Could it be a smuggler's cache?

Eagerly she went toward them, squeezing between the mounds of luggage.

One look, and she saw that she was mistaken. The origin was the United States, and the destination was Kuala Lumpur. The packages hadn't come in from Korea at all.

"You struck out," she muttered under her breath.

Hurrying, Nancy weaved her way to the open door.

She was halfway to the door when she saw a man's arm—in a black flight jacket—flash across the opening and grab the outer door handle. He jerked twice, trying to slide the door shut.

"Wait!" Nancy called. "I'm in here!"

But instead of waiting, the man jerked harder, slamming the door shut with such finality that Nancy gasped. He'd shut her in on purpose!

Nancy stumbled the rest of the way across the compartment and pounded her fist against the door. "Open up!" she screamed. "Open the door!"

To her horror, she felt a sudden trembling of the plane as the engines started to rev. The noise grew to unbelievable proportions.

Nancy stood frozen to the spot. The plane was taking off!

Chapter

Five

NANCY SEARCHED WILDLY for the catch that would open the door. She had to get out before the plane started moving. Otherwise she'd have to fly in a nonpressurized, unheated compartment all the way to Singapore!

"Let me out!" she yelled, banging her fist against the door. "I'm in here! Let me out!" There was no way anyone could hear her over the plane's engines, but she had to try. "Help! Somebody help me!" she called again.

The plane gave a short jerk, and she nearly lost her footing. Holding on, she felt the plane begin to back away from the gate!

Nancy's self-reliance had helped her out of some pretty tight scrapes before. Now her mind raced, searching for an escape. The door was operated by a lever above it, but she couldn't reach it. She needed something to stand on.

She grabbed the nearest box and pulled it over. She strained for the lever, but the plane's movement threw her down. Nancy scrambled up again. This time, her hand had actually connected with the handle when the plane suddenly stopped moving. Instead of backing up, it was rolling forward again. The engines were winding down!

Collapsing in relief, Nancy sank against the hull. She didn't know why, but the plane was going back to the gate.

When Nancy heard voices outside, she banged against the door and yelled again. Then she heard the slam of the portable staircase being shoved against the side of the plane. Footsteps came clambering up the rungs.

"Nancy! We're coming!" she heard Sean yell.

Her legs were decidedly shaky as the door was thrown open and Sean and another man rushed inside. "Nancy, are you all right?" Sean asked. His face was pale and set.

"I'm fine. Now." Nancy gave him a crooked smile. "How did you get them to stop the plane?"

"I didn't. The mechanical problems that have been going on all day still aren't fixed. They couldn't risk putting the plane in the air again."

Realizing what a close call she had had, Nancy grew sober. This case was growing more dangerous every minute!

"You'd better get out of here, miss," the man with Sean told her.

Nancy went down the stairway, lost in thought. Who had shut her in the plane? Had it been an accident? If so, why hadn't the man answered her when she had told him she was inside?

"I'm so glad you're all right," Sean said as they walked inside the building. "When I saw that plane backing away, I nearly died."

Nancy smiled her thanks. "By any chance did you see the man who shut me in?" she asked.

Sean shook his head, frowning. "No. I wasn't around. I got called into the terminal. It was probably just one of the handlers who didn't know you were inside."

"Well, if it was, he must be hard of hearing. I yelled and yelled when he started to shut the door, but he went ahead and shut it anyway."

Sean stared at her in disbelief. "He couldn't have heard you. No one would deliberately shut you in!"

Why was Sean trying so hard to dismiss her narrow escape as an accident? "He had to have heard me," Nancy said definitely. "He *knew* I was in there!"

"Look, Nancy." Sean stopped short. "I'm going to be perfectly honest with you. I don't believe there's really any smuggling going on, or that Rod was murdered. I'm just playing along with this because Jennifer's so wrapped up in the idea of being a detective. And I'm about ready to quit doing that!"

Nancy blinked. "But what about the vase? What about the threatening note?"

Sean continued as if he hadn't heard her. "I don't want Jennifer involved anymore. The vase has got to be a fake. Rod wouldn't have owned something like that. And the note . . ." He shrugged. "I don't know. Maybe having a detective around just makes people nervous."

Nancy could understand Sean's wish to keep Jennifer safe, but privately she thought his reasoning was pretty weak. "I tend to take threatening notes seriously," she told him.

"Then maybe you should go back to River Heights," Sean said flatly. "If there is something going on, you're in way over your head."

"I can't leave yet, Sean," Nancy said, shoving her hands into her pockets. "Not until I get to the bottom of this thing."

Sean's jaw tightened. "It's your funeral," he said.

Nancy grimaced at his choice of words. "Who was it who called you into the terminal when I was inside the plane?"

"One of the guys told me I'd been paged. So I went inside to answer the call. By the time I got there they'd hung up. I figured it was probably Jennifer."

"Or it could have been a ruse to get you away from the plane," Nancy pointed out.

Sean looked as if he didn't want to believe her. His face grew pale again. "Look, let's keep this from Jennifer, okay? I don't want her getting into this any more than she already has."

"It might be a better idea just to level with her," Nancy said.

Sean sent her a look she couldn't decipher. "You're the detective," he muttered, and then he wouldn't say anything more.

Once inside the building Nancy went to watch the customs agents search through passengers' luggage. She realized then that nothing could have escaped their professional attention. If there was any smuggling going on, the goods weren't going through customs.

Sean was waiting for Nancy at the door to the upper stairway. They headed back to meet Jennifer. With Sean's pointed silence, conversation was practically nonexistent. A thought kept creeping into Nancy's head—one she didn't even want to consider. Could Sean's reason for wanting her off the case be that *he* was involved in the smuggling ring?

Nancy glanced at him. He was so handsome, so cool and collected. What if he'd been the one to lock her inside the plane? If he were part of the smuggling operation, he had opportunity *and* motive!

Nancy tried to shake her thoughts away. Sean couldn't be involved. He just couldn't!

When they finally met up with Jennifer again, she was almost dancing with impatience. "Well, it's about time!" she snapped. "What happened? Did you find anything out?"

Nancy could feel Sean's eyes boring into her back. She wanted to tell Jen everything, but for the moment just said, "I didn't find any evidence of smuggling."

"You look kind of funny," Jennifer insisted. "*Something* must have happened."

With his easy manner, Sean put his arm around Jennifer and steered her toward the door. "Nothing happened. Come on. Let's forget all this mystery stuff for a while and go get that pizza."

Twisting her neck around to look at Nancy, Jen asked, "Nothing happened?"

"We weren't going to talk about the mystery anymore, remember?" Nancy's tone was deliberately light. "Let's just go get Bess."

With a sheepish smile, Jennifer said, "Right. I forgot. Sorry I've been acting so lousy, Nancy. It's just because I want to help."

"No problem," Nancy assured her friend.

Jennifer's already kind of upset with me, Nancy thought. How will she feel if I prove that her boyfriend's somehow involved? What'll happen to our friendship then?

It was a question Nancy didn't want to think about.

The pizza parlor Sean chose wasn't far from the airport. It was a regular hangout for the employees of all the airlines.

"How's it going, Bess?" Nancy asked her friend.

"It's terrible!"

"Terrible?" Nancy repeated. "You've got to be kidding!" Then, seeing that Bess was completely serious, she asked, "Why? What's wrong?"

"What's wrong? Everything's wrong! There's so much to remember I'll never get it all straight," Bess wailed. "Tomorrow we're on a simulated flight, and then we have an emergency landing, and *I'm* supposed to help these people off the plane!"

"Here." Nancy slid the pizza Bess's way. "Have another piece. It'll make you feel better."

"No way." Bess shook her head mournfully. "Any more and I won't be able to fit into my uniform." She wagged her finger in front of Nancy's nose. "The next time I let you talk me into a vacation where a mystery's involved, remind me that it'll be all *work*."

"Not all work," Jennifer said sympathetically. "I'm going to introduce you to Mark on Friday, remember?"

Bess, who had been eyeing the pizza, looked up. "Who's Mark?"

51

"The cute blond copilot I was telling you about. I even told him about you."

"You did?" Bess's eyes widened. "What did he say?"

"He said he was looking forward to Friday," she said.

Bess grabbed her diet soda. "I need fortification, then," she said, "if I'm going to pass this class."

"Me, too." Nancy stood up.

"Where are you going?" Bess asked.

"To get fortification. I'm going to order another pizza."

"It's all a diabolical plan to ruin me," Bess moaned, covering her face with her hands. Everyone at the table laughed.

Later, after they'd eaten all they could and Jennifer and Sean had wandered over to the jukebox, Nancy said to Bess in a low voice, "I've got problems."

"What kind of problems?"

As Nancy told her about her "unscheduled" flight, Bess's eyes grew as round as saucers. "Nancy, this is getting really dangerous," she whispered. "Someone wants you out of the picture!"

"I know. But that's not the half of it. Ever since I got locked in the baggage compartment, I've had these terrible suspicions about Sean."

"Sean!"

"Shhh." Nancy glanced over her shoulder—but Sean and Jennifer only had eyes for each other.

"You've got to be wrong," Bess protested. "Sean *can't* be involved!"

"I know, I know. But think about it, Bess. Someone has to have known my every move. Besides you and Jennifer, only Sean, Mr. Talbot, and Miranda knew anything about me."

"What about Miranda, then?" Bess asked. "Rod gave *her* the vase."

Nancy sighed as she poured herself another glass of soda. "Miranda offered the vase as evidence before I even had any idea about it. Besides, she's off on a trip to Hawaii. She won't be back until tomorrow. I don't see how she could be involved."

"Then it's Mr. Talbot," Bess said defensively. "It can't be Sean."

"I hope you're right, but if it's Preston Talbot, then we're all in real trouble," Nancy said grimly. "Especially Jennifer."

Bess shivered. "Why Jennifer?"

"Because she's so wrapped up in the adventure of it all that she's forgotten the danger. She's jumping the gun all the time. I'm afraid she's going to get hurt."

Nancy took a deep breath. "If Mr. Talbot's involved, then he's just using us until he can find a way to get rid of us. No one's safe. Not you, me, Sean, Miranda, or Jennifer."

"So what do we do?" Bess asked fearfully. "Honestly, Nancy, you're giving me the creeps."

Nancy knew exactly how Bess felt. She didn't like thinking Mr. Talbot was the culprit any more than she liked imagining her friends as enemies. "We just have to be careful and solve this mystery," she said. "Either that, or one of us might end up dead."

Chapter

Six

THE NEXT MORNING, after Bess had left to continue with her flight training, Nancy spent a couple of hours thinking over the whole situation. Who had shut her inside the plane? Was it the same person who had thrown the rock with the threatening note? Or was it someone else?

The note on the rock really puzzled her. She had assumed it was simply a threat, but now she wondered if it was a warning instead. Maybe someone wasn't afraid *of* her as much as they were afraid *for* her.

Nancy thought that over as she drove her car back to the airport the next day. Of the people who had known she was coming to Seattle, Mr. Talbot had been inside the room when the rock was thrown. Jennifer and Bess had been with her. That left Sean or Miranda as the hooded figure Nancy'd seen—and Miranda had been on a flight that day.

"I'll have to check what time she got in," Nancy said to herself.

With the help of Celia, a friendly management trainee Nancy had met the day before, she checked Miranda's flight schedule.

"Flight one thirty-three got in at twenty-five after four the day before yesterday," Celia told her. "The plane was late."

"Four twenty-five," Nancy repeated thoughtfully. There was no way Miranda could have thrown the rock, escaped, and still have beaten Nancy, Jennifer, and Bess to the apartment.

That left Sean.

"Or someone else you know nothing about," Nancy murmured.

"Pardon?" Celia looked up.

"I was just talking to myself." Nancy smiled. "It's nothing new, believe me."

Nancy said goodbye and went through the door that led to Victory's inner offices, headed downstairs, and began walking through the lower level to the baggage-sorting area to face Grant Sweeney again.

About halfway there she noticed a sign she hadn't noticed the day before. "Customs," she read thoughtfully, looking down the short hallway to a locked door. So the customs station was right next to Victory's baggage-sorting room. Could this be the way the smugglers brought goods in to bypass customs?

Nancy walked to the locked door. It was secured by a chain and deadbolt. In bold letters a sign stated clearly that no one but customs personnel was allowed inside.

Nancy examined the heavy chain closely. "No security risk here," she muttered. She didn't see how anyone could get through that door without a key—and even then the customs personnel inside would be alerted.

Nancy then went to find Grant Sweeney. Sweeney certainly didn't want her around, and Nancy figured there must be a reason. Maybe Sweeney had been the hooded figure!

But Grant Sweeney didn't know I was coming to Seattle, Nancy reminded herself. Who else could have thrown the rock besides Sean?

The baggage room was much the same as it had been the day before. Nancy recognized some of the guys, and several others came over and introduced themselves.

Suddenly Paul appeared. When he saw Nancy, he came over and put his arm around her shoulders.

Grinning, Nancy removed his arm. "I'd love to talk, but I really need to find Sweeney."

Paul sighed and threw a hand dramatically

across his heart. "All right. I'll let you go. But if I die of a broken heart, let it be on your conscience." Then he added, "Sweeney's office is that-a-way." He pointed to the rear of the room.

"Thanks. You've been a real help."

"Don't mention it. And the name's Paul, remember? By the way, what's yours?"

"Nancy Drew."

She headed for the back door, but halfway there she decided on another plan of attack.

"Oh, Paul—" she said thoughtfully, returning.

"Love of my life, you've come back to me!" Paul declared, throwing open his arms and rushing toward her. His friends hooted with laughter.

"Get serious," Nancy said, hiding a smile. "I need to talk to you."

"I am serious. I'm always serious. This is a serious talk? Okay, good. Yes, I'll marry you."

"When you have a break," Nancy said, managing to keep a straight face, "I'd like to ask you a few questions."

"Break starts—right about—" Paul looked at his watch, silently counting the passing seconds. "Now!" Grabbing his coat, he came over to her side and said, "Ask away. I'm yours forever—or fifteen minutes—whichever comes first."

Nancy sighed. She had probably picked the wrong guy for getting information! But she forged on. "Were you working yesterday?"

"Uh-huh. All day. Has anyone ever told you you have the most fantastic hair?"

"Yesterday," Nancy tried again, "I came here with Sean, and then I went outside to look in the baggage compartment of one of the seven forty-sevens."

"You did?" For the first time Paul dropped his act and looked at Nancy seriously.

She nodded. "And then someone shut the door —with me inside. The plane's engines started. For a moment I thought I was heading for Singapore whether I wanted to or not."

Paul was looking at Nancy as if she were crazy. "What were you doing in there in the first place?"

"Just looking. Can you remember who was working here yesterday afternoon?"

"What are you, some kind of detective or something?"

"Or something." Nancy smiled.

Paul opened his mouth to respond, then seemed to think better of it. A frown creased his brow. "All the guys that are here today were here yesterday. Except—Sean's not here today. He's at Talbot's management trainee courses."

"*Mr. Talbot's* management trainee courses?" Nancy was quiet then. The one link between Rod, Sean, and Talbot was the management trainee program. Was it a coincidence?

"Anything else you want to know?"

Nancy looked into Paul's boyish face. She was glad she'd met him. "Sean told me he got paged late yesterday afternoon. He said one of the guys here sent for him."

"That's right." Paul nodded. "Grant told me Sean had a page. He asked me to go get him."

"You were the one who got Sean?"

"Yeah. Why?"

Nancy didn't enlighten him. She just gave him a smile, thanked him for his help, and went in the direction of Grant Sweeney's office. This section of the airport was poorly heated, and the floors were concrete. Nancy blew on her hands as she walked down the chilly corridor.

Grant Sweeney's name wasn't on the door she took to be his office. A huge sign marked "Private" was the only decoration. Knocking loudly, Nancy waited for a response. When none came, she twisted the knob. It was locked.

This, she decided, was a prime time to do some undercover searching on her own. Digging through her purse, Nancy found a paper clip. She unfolded it and inserted it in the hole in the lock, but before she had time to pick the lock, the door suddenly swung inward—and Nancy tumbled forward. As her gaze traveled up, she saw Grant Sweeney towering over her, holding a wrench high above her head!

Chapter

Seven

FOR A MOMENT Nancy was utterly transfixed. She couldn't believe Grant Sweeney would actually hit her, but his eyes were dark and angry, his knuckles white as his fingers tightened around the wrench.

Nancy held her breath.

Slowly he lowered the wrench. "Sorry," he said gruffly. "I've just been taking extra precautions with all this talk about smugglers. I thought you were trying to break in."

"Who said anything about smugglers?" she asked, her heart pounding as she stood up inside the door frame. As far as she knew, that bit of information was still confidential. Nancy had been careful not to mention it when she had questioned the Victory employees.

"Well, you did. You were—you were talking about that vase—"

"Which vase? I didn't mention any one vase in particular."

"Down by those crates in baggage," Grant insisted. "You were talking about some vase."

"I didn't mention smuggling," Nancy said softly.

"Say, who *are* you?" Grant demanded, bristling. "I don't think I like your questions. And I don't have to answer them."

He moved to slam the door in her face, but Nancy quickly shoved her foot inside the opening. She wasn't ready to end their conversation yet.

"If you don't want your foot smashed, you'd better move it. *Now!*" he growled.

Desperately Nancy blocked the door with her shoulder. "I'm a friend of Mr. Talbot's. He gave me clearance to come and check on security."

"Well, everything's secure here. So you can beat it," he said.

"What gave you the idea about smuggling?" Nancy insisted. "Did you see something? Overhear something?" Her gut instincts told her Grant was involved. He had to be getting his information somehow, and she had to know how.

Grant's eyes narrowed. "I just heard it around, that's all." His big, beefy hand began slowly shutting the door.

There was nothing more she could do—unless she wanted him smashing her foot or shoulder. Nancy was forced to back away. "Someone must have told you," she said. "I just want to know who it was."

Just before the door closed in her face, she got the impression of a cold smile twitching the corner of Sweeney's mouth. "Why don't you ask your friend Talbot?"

The door slammed shut. Nancy stared at the panels for several moments. Ask Mr. Talbot? Was Grant giving her a clue? Or was he just trying to mislead her?

Well, what about Preston Talbot? As president of the airline, it would be so easy for him to run illicit goods through Victory. There was no one above him to question his authority. And if Mr. Talbot was involved, Sweeney had to be involved, too. *He* must have been the hooded figure. But would Grant Sweeney point the finger at Preston Talbot if the two were working together?

At least Nancy was relieved that the trail had turned away from Sean. Now all she had to do was prove the connection between Sweeney and Talbot and that would cinch it!

As Nancy rode the elevator up to Mr. Talbot's office, questions kept circling through her mind. Just how much contraband was getting smuggled past customs? And how was it getting through? She knew how tight the restrictions were. As far as she could tell, the only feasible way to bring in stolen merchandise was to bypass customs. But how was it being done?

Still lost in thought, Nancy knocked on Mr. Talbot's door.

"Come on in," he called. "It's open."

Nancy stepped through, and Preston Talbot looked up from his desk. "Just the person I wanted to see," he said. "I've been worrying about this smuggling thing day and night. Have you made any progress?"

Nancy licked her lips. She wasn't certain how much to reveal. "Some," she admitted evasively.

"It's true, then?" Mr. Talbot asked quickly. "Someone's using Victory Airlines to smuggle in valuables?"

"All the evidence points that way."

"It's got to be stopped!" Mr. Talbot slammed his fist against his desk, his face turning dark red. "I've built up the reputation of this airline single-handedly. I won't let anyone ruin it! I want these smugglers caught and put away!"

"Is there anyone at Victory with enough power and flexibility to run a major smuggling ring?" Nancy knew she was playing a dangerous game of cat and mouse, but there was no other way to get the kind of information she needed.

Mr. Talbot seemed taken aback. "Well, I suppose anyone in upper management could. But no one would. Victory's our whole life."

Nancy nodded, remembering Paul's remark that the management trainee program had been Mr.

Talbot's idea. If he *was* behind the smuggling ring, could the program be a front? A way to bring in new recruits to join the gang? If so, where did that leave Sean?

"One of us . . ." Mr. Talbot said reflectively, shaking his head. "That's a frightening thought. Ask Blake Maxell, the district manager, about which employees could be involved. He'd know better than I would."

"I'll do that." Nancy slung her purse over her shoulder and headed for the door. "Oh, by the way," she said, her hand on the knob, "I'd like to check through some airline records. Is there someone who could help me?"

"Any of the ticketing agents could help you get what you need from the computer." He smiled tightly. "And if any of them give you a hard time, have them call me."

"Thanks."

Nancy left his office with mixed feelings. Preston Talbot seemed truly concerned about the reputation of the airline. But it could all be an act. She supposed talking to Blake Maxell would be a good idea, but that would mean one more person who'd know what she was up to. Deciding to postpone that talk until later, she went to the airline ticketing desk. She was relieved to see Celia there. At least she could count on Celia to be helpful!

Nancy walked up to her and said, "I need some background information on Victory. Mr. Talbot told me to come down here and ask one of the ticketing agents to help me."

"Your wish is my command." Celia's lips curved in a friendly smile. "What do you need to know?"

Nancy couldn't help feeling a little guilty. Now that she'd decided on the management trainee program as the source for possible smugglers, she was even including Celia as a suspect. But it couldn't be helped.

"I need to know everything," Nancy told Celia. She began by asking basic questions about Victory's operation—how many planes they had, a list of all their destinations, how many offices worldwide, how many employees, and so on.

Celia punched into the computer, pulling up the data Nancy had requested. While Celia's fingers were flying over the computer keyboard and the printer was spewing out sheets of paper, Nancy casually asked, "How do you like the management trainee program?"

"It's the best," Celia said enthusiastically. "We have district offices all over the world, but because Preston Talbot's in Seattle, the program's most effective here. A friend of mine went straight from the program to become assistant to the district manager in Taiwan!"

"Wow." Keeping her eyes on the lines of data on the computer screen, Nancy asked, "Did Mr. Talbot recommend your friend for the job?"

"I think so. No, wait—maybe it was Blake

Maxell. I'm not sure. I just hope I get a job half as good as that one when I'm through with training."

When the printer had finished, Celia ripped off the papers. "Is that everything?" she asked, handing the bundle to Nancy.

Remembering the 747 clue from Rod, Nancy said, "Just a minute. Could I get a list of all Victory's seven forty-seven planes and their destinations?"

"Sure," she said and quickly punched a series of buttons, and the information began coming off the printer.

Once Nancy had all the data she needed, she thanked Celia and headed for a quiet spot to study it. She flipped through page after page, groaning when she realized she was going to be spending most of the next day reading through all of it. After a few minutes she shoved the bulk of it aside and grabbed the list of Victory's 747s.

The list was surprisingly long. Most of the huge jets flew overseas, but one of them was currently on a Seattle–New York route. She didn't see how it could be used for smuggling goods from the Orient.

"The trouble is I've got too much information," Nancy said, sighing as she folded up the printouts.

She stopped into the airport café that was located on a balcony above the main terminal. From there she had a bird's-eye view of all Victory comings and goings. Nancy ordered a taco salad and tea and sat down to eat, her eyes on the single door that led to Victory's inner offices and the baggage handling room.

She wondered how Bess's second day of training was going. By the next evening Bess would be a full-fledged flight attendant. Nancy felt a pang of envy.

Nancy finished her meal, glanced at her watch, and saw that it was almost two. The morning shift ended at three-thirty, and, she had learned, Grant would be done that day at that time.

She spent the next hour reading through the printouts again, then gathered her things and headed to the employee parking lot.

Her rental car was right where she had parked it: near the center walkway and not too far from the exit gate. After climbing inside, Nancy clicked on her seat belt and flexed her hands around the wheel. She wasn't going to let Grant Sweeney get away.

There he was, walking across the parking lot! Nancy slumped down in the seat, her pulse racing. Out of the corner of her eye she watched him pass right beside her car. He didn't even glance her way. Peeking up, she saw him climb into a shiny red pickup with oversize wheels and a roll bar. "You're going to be easy to see in that rig," she said aloud, smiling, her eyes fixed on the red truck.

Sweeney pulled out of the parking lot and headed straight for the freeway. Nancy followed, keeping several cars between them. Then he turned off the freeway toward Seattle's city center, weaving through the late-afternoon traffic.

Nancy was careful to stay in a different lane, a few cars back, following in his blind spot. But then a red light stopped Grant. There were no cars in front of Nancy, so she had to move up next to him. Desperately she tried to hang back, but horns blared from behind her.

That was all it took. Grant looked over, spied Nancy, and tore through the red light, tires spinning.

The oncoming traffic forced Nancy to wait. When the light changed, she stamped on the accelerator. She was pleased to see that Grant had gotten stopped again one block in front of her.

She pulled up two cars behind him. When the light changed he took off in another direction, and she followed.

They drove farther and farther from city center, heading toward the industrial area. Nancy could catch glimpses of Seattle's waterfront between the buildings, but her eyes remained glued to the road and the red pickup in front of her.

Sweeney took a hard right. Nancy hung on his tail as they zigzagged through the hilly streets. Nancy was getting confused. Hadn't they just gone this way? Why was he circling around?

Sweeney's rig bumped over a series of railroad tracks. More cautiously, Nancy started to cross them.

Suddenly bells sounded and the black-and-white gates ahead began to lower. Stepping on the gas, Sweeney sped through them—and Nancy's car was still racing forward.

She slammed on her brakes at the gate. But the rear of her car fish-tailed and began sliding sideways toward the tracks.

Nancy looked over her shoulder and screamed. The train was barreling straight down on her car!

Chapter
Eight

NANCY DESPERATELY TRIED to keep the car from sliding. The train's horn blasted again, long and loud. Frantically she twisted the wheel. Her car came to a shuddering halt—inches from disaster—as the train thundered by.

Nancy ran her hands through her hair and closed her eyes. Grant Sweeney had led her into a trap, trying to kill her!

As the last car clattered by, Nancy turned her car around and started back toward Jennifer's apartment. She had had enough for one day.

Jennifer was at the apartment when Nancy got there. "You look beat. Did something happen today? Tell me!"

The last thing Nancy wanted to do was get into a major discussion about the case with Jennifer. Luckily she was saved from answering when Miranda burst through the door.

"Whew! I'm exhausted," she said. "That was the longest flight from Honolulu I've ever been on."

"Well, it couldn't have been because Linda Cotilla was on it. She was on *my* flight." Jennifer rolled her eyes. "What a disaster. Don't tell Bess, but Linda's been assigned to the Seattle–Los Angeles trip. She's going to be on our flight tomorrow, too."

Miranda shook her head. "Poor Bess."

"I tell you what—let's make cookies," Jennifer suggested, heading for the kitchen.

"Great idea," Miranda and Nancy seconded, falling in behind her.

While the second batch of coconut macaroons was in the oven, Sean and Bess arrived. A huge smile was spread across Bess's face.

"I passed!" she said triumphantly. "No problem."

"Tomorrow's the real test," Miranda said. "You're on a flight with Cotilla the Hun."

"Oh, no. Really?" Bess looked around at them. "I hope you're joking."

"She can't be that bad," Nancy said, trying to assure her, but Miranda and Jennifer chorused together, "Oh, yes, she can!"

"Thanks for being so encouraging," Bess said, deflated.

"But—remember Mark, that copilot I was telling you about?" Jennifer asked.

"Uh-huh," Bess said without real interest.

"He's on our flight tomorrow, too."

"Yeah?" Bess sounded more interested.

"We'll have a couple of hours in L.A. Maybe we can all get together for lunch or something," Jennifer said.

"*Lunch*. Great. Just what I need. Pizza last night, hamburgers the night before, cookies now —I'll be a blimp before we get back to River Heights!"

"Don't worry. I'm making a chef salad for dinner," Miranda said. "I was just heading out to the store. You can load up on cookies and then graze on salad."

"My kind of diet," Bess said with a contented sigh.

They spent the rest of the evening relaxing and talking. Nancy was glad that the conversation had shifted away from her investigation. But after Miranda and Bess had gone to bed, Jennifer brought it up again.

"What happened today, Nancy?" she asked in the kitchen as they were putting the last dishes away. "Did you make any progress on the case? Who did you talk to? Did you see Mr. Talbot?"

Nancy felt boxed into a corner. Sean's eyes were on her, and she hardly knew what to say. "I think you were right about the smuggling, Jennifer," she finally admitted reluctantly.

"Really?" Jennifer sounded beside herself with excitement. "I knew it! I just knew it! Oh, I wish I could have been there with you. I'm absolutely *dying* to help!"

"Look, Jen," Sean said, shrugging into his coat. "Nancy's the detective. Why don't you just let her do her job and get on with it?"

Jennifer paused, taken aback. "What? This is happening to Victory, Sean! Our airline! Don't you even care?"

"Of course I care. But I'm not crazy enough to think I can do a better job than Nancy. You asked her to come here and solve this thing. Well, why don't you just let her do it?"

"I think I can handle myself, thanks," Jennifer said, her voice rising. "And who made you my keeper?" Jennifer demanded furiously. "You don't have to look out for me!"

"Fine." Sean cut her off and strode out the front door, slamming it behind him.

Tears filled Jennifer's eyes. "What does he know, anyway?" she said.

"But you love him, Jen," Nancy said. "This case isn't worth losing Sean."

"You're only saying that because you don't want me involved in your case, either," Jennifer said, dashing the tears out of her eyes.

"That's not true. I just don't want you to lose Sean. He's worried about you because he cares."

"If Sean really cared, he would be more interested," Jennifer declared. "The way he's acting, it's as if he doesn't want us to learn the truth! Oh, forget it," Jennifer said curtly. "I'm going to bed. I'll see you tomorrow."

Nancy walked into the living room and looked at Bess. "I'm really worried about Jennifer and Sean," Nancy said quietly.

"Me, too. I'd hate to see them break up. You don't think Sean's involved, do you?" Bess asked.

"I really don't know." As briefly as possible Nancy told Bess about tailing Grant Sweeney and how she had almost gotten killed at the railroad tracks. "I don't know about Sean," she repeated, "but Sweeney's in it up to his eyeballs."

Bess's eyes were terrified. "Can't you do something to protect yourself, Nan?" she gasped.

"Oh, I'll be fine," answered Nancy, trying to speak casually. "Now you get some sleep, Bess. You've got a big day ahead of you."

In a few minutes Nancy heard her friend's even breathing. She went back into the kitchen and put the teapot on the stove.

A few moments later Miranda wandered into the kitchen. She stopped short when she saw Nancy. "I thought everyone was asleep," she said, yawning, her red hair a tousled cloud around her head.

"I knew I couldn't sleep," Nancy admitted. "Too many things on my mind."

"Me, too." Miranda frowned. "I just keep thinking about Rod and this smuggling thing." She shivered. "What should I do about the vase? I don't like keeping it here."

"I was planning to do some research at the library on the vase, but I haven't had time," Nancy said, her brow puckering.

The teapot whistled, and Nancy poured them each a cup of tea.

"Thanks," Miranda said, smiling. "With service like this, you can stay as long as you like."

"I'll remember that." Nancy smiled, then grew sober. "Maybe I should take a look at that vase again," she said.

"Okay. I have it in a suitcase in my room." Miranda led the way back to her bedroom. Pulling the suitcase out of her closet, she gasped. "The lock's broken!"

"What about the vase?" Nancy asked, her heart sinking.

Miranda threw open the suitcase. "It's gone. Oh, Nancy, someone's stolen it!" she cried.

Chapter
Nine

THE TWO GIRLS stared at the empty suitcase. "Who could have taken it?" Miranda asked.

Nancy had a few ideas about who—but she kept them to herself.

Miranda's cries had woken Jennifer and Bess. They came running to her bedroom. "What's going on?" Jennifer demanded.

"Our smugglers have discovered we're on to them," Nancy said grimly. "Someone stole the vase from Miranda's suitcase."

"Who? How?" Jennifer looked frightened.

"I don't know."

"But who knew about the vase besides us and Sean?" Miranda asked.

"Mr. Talbot knew," Jennifer said. "But he's on our side." At Nancy's silence, she asked, "Well, isn't he? I mean, he is the president."

"We can't rule out anyone at this point." Nancy tried to sound matter-of-fact.

"The president of the airline?" Jennifer looked at Nancy as if she'd lost her mind. "Come on. Why would he risk everything he's worked for?"

"Power. Money," Nancy answered. "It's just a theory."

"Yeah, but your theories have a way of becoming fact," Bess pointed out. "I bet it *is* Mr. Talbot."

But Nancy's thoughts had turned to Grant Sweeney. In his presence she'd mentioned Chinese vases in general. But she hadn't said that Rod had given one to Miranda. Would Grant have searched their apartment in the hopes of finding the vase on that slim bit of information? Or had he learned from Mr. Talbot that Miranda had the vase? That is, if he *did* take it, she reminded herself.

"I don't like this," Miranda said, wrapping her arms around herself and looking nervously over her shoulder.

"That vase was the only solid piece of evidence we had, and now it's gone." Nancy sighed. "It must have been the real thing after all. The smugglers brought it in from the Orient. And Rod probably lifted it from an illegal shipment, then gave it to Miranda."

"Could we talk about this in the morning?" Bess asked, stifling a yawn. "I'm bushed, and my first day in the air is tomorrow."

The others agreed and went to bed also.

Nancy spent most of the next morning going over the Victory printouts. Around noon she drove to the airport. She wanted to check with Blake Maxell about who had enough pull in the company to organize a smuggling ring and keep it under wraps.

She was going to ask Celia where his office was, but stopped short when she saw the man himself, talking to Celia at the flight desk.

"You can't afford to make mistakes like that," he was saying in a flat, hard tone. "One more time and you're fired!"

Celia looked about ready to cry. "I'm sorry, Mr. Maxell," she answered. "The computer went down while I was changing the reservation. By the time it came back up again, the seats were gone."

"I told you to make that reservation yesterday! You should have done it the instant I told you to!"

"I—I know."

"Book me another flight to New York as soon as possible. See if you can manage *that* without making a mistake."

He stalked off toward the door to the offices.

Nancy walked quickly up to the counter. "That was Blake Maxell?" she asked, inclining her head in the direction Maxell had just taken.

"Yes." Celia managed a weak smile. "His reservation slipped my mind after the computer went down. If I make any more mistakes like that one, I can kiss this job goodbye."

"I think he overreacted," Nancy said. "It was an honest mistake."

"No, he had every right to be angry with me."

Celia seemed so upset that Nancy dropped the subject. But she had lost her zeal to meet with Maxell. Instead she talked to several of the other management trainees. Late in the afternoon she ran into Paul, and he insisted she spend his break with him.

"I refuse to give up on you," he said. "So how about tonight? We could hit a movie, or go out to dinner, whatever."

"I can't, Paul. Really. I've got too much to do."

"It's Sean, isn't it?" Paul guessed. "Something's going on between you two."

"No way! Sean's in love with Jennifer," Nancy pointed out to Paul, "and besides, I've got a boyfriend back home."

"I don't know about your boyfriend, but I can tell you that Sean and Jennifer are kaput. And I think you're the reason."

"That's not even worth answering!" she snapped.

"I heard Sean tell one of the guys that things haven't been the same between him and Jennifer since you came to Seattle."

"You don't understand. It's all because of

this—" Nancy caught herself before she said "smuggling ring."

As if Sean had heard them talking about him, he appeared just then. Seeing Nancy and Paul, he hesitated, then came toward them.

"Well, guess who's looking for you," Paul said sardonically. "This must be my cue to leave."

Nancy's eyes flashed with indignation, but Paul took off before she had a chance to set him straight.

"So how's it going?" Sean asked without much interest.

Putting Paul out of her mind, Nancy said, "I'm making some progress—I think. But Victory seems to be a close-knit operation. If anybody knows anything, they're not talking."

"Give up, Nancy," Sean said suddenly. "It's not worth it. Look at what's happened since you got here. You practically ended up flying to Singapore. Then chasing Grant Sweeney, you almost got yourself killed!"

Nancy's blood ran cold. "How did you know about me chasing Sweeney?"

Sean stopped short, his jaw tightening. "Oh, so now you're looking at me, huh? Am I a suspect? Well, for your information, Bess told me when I saw her this morning before her flight. You're a nuisance. I heard Grant Sweeney complaining about you, too. So go away, Nancy. Do us all a big favor and take the first flight back to River Heights!"

Chapter
Ten

IT WAS GROWING dark as Nancy pulled up to Jennifer's apartment complex. Jennifer's car was already parked in its usual spot, which meant Jen and Bess were back from their flight.

Nancy let herself inside the apartment in time to hear Jennifer saying, "It's nothing to worry about, Bess. She treats everybody that way."

"I don't want to go back tomorrow. I can't stand people like that," Bess wailed.

"People like what?" Nancy asked, shrugging out of her coat.

"Oh, Nancy. Cotilla the Hun was even worse than they said! She ran me ragged—barking orders, yelling at me. I nearly dropped a tray in a passenger's lap, I was so upset." Bess shuddered.

"If it's really so bad, don't go back up," Nancy said. "We're supposed to be having fun, too."

"You know I'm not going to let you down, Nancy. I'll go back up tomorrow, and I'll put a smile on my face if it kills me!"

Bess's loyalty touched Nancy. "Thanks," she said.

"What's *with* that woman?" Nancy asked more to herself than to her friends. "I wonder if she knows Bess is working undercover?"

Jennifer's eyes widened. "You think Linda's involved in the smuggling ring?" she asked eagerly.

"All I know is what you've told me—and that's that Linda's been unusually short-tempered and nervous. Sounds to me as though she's under some kind of heavy pressure."

"Wow." Jennifer sank onto the couch. "So that's why she's been such a bear these last few weeks!"

"Remember, we don't know anything for sure yet," Nancy put in hastily. "It could be something else entirely."

"If Linda's involved, then she's working with Mr. Talbot," Jennifer said, her eyes narrowing thoughtfully. "And Rod Fullerton was in on it, too. This operation is getting bigger and bigger."

Jennifer had tossed off her black jacket, and now she was examining the pale pink polish on her nails. "Did you run into Sean at all?" she asked. Her voice was casual, but Nancy could tell how much she was hurting.

"As a matter of fact, I did."

Jennifer looked up quickly. Then she glanced away. "So how was he?"

"Miserable. I think he misses you."

"Sean Richmond is only interested in advancing up the corporate ladder. And he doesn't care how he does it!"

Nancy drew a deep breath. Sean and Preston Talbot did seem to know each other fairly well. Was it because of the management trainee program, or something else? Nancy hadn't forgotten the way they had cut off their conversation when she and Jennifer had entered Mr. Talbot's office.

Was Jennifer right in thinking Sean would do *anything* for his career?

"What are you thinking about?" Jennifer asked suddenly.

Startled, Nancy said, "Oh, nothing in particular."

"You were thinking about Sean, weren't you? What is it, Nancy? What do you know?" When Nancy didn't say anything, she burst out, "It's not Sean, you know. He doesn't have anything to do with the smuggling ring, so just get that idea out of your head!"

Before Nancy could answer, though, Bess came to her defense. "You just said he'd do anything to further his career," she pointed out.

"I didn't mean that! Sean wouldn't do anything like that. He's just—he's just—" Jennifer suddenly burst into tears and ran into her bedroom.

Bess's lips parted in dismay. "I feel terrible!"

"So do I." Nancy sank down on the couch. "It feels as if everything's going from bad to worse. The worst thing of all is that I *do* suspect Sean a little. And having Jennifer know it makes me feel like a heel."

"You can't help that," Bess said philosophically. "Just keep plugging away. You'll figure it all out. You always do."

The rest of the evening passed without incident. Jennifer came out of her room in a few minutes. And when Nancy suggested they all go out and get something to eat, she went along with them. But she wasn't her usual self, and when they got back to the apartment she went straight to bed.

"She's really hurting about Sean," Bess said as she and Nancy made some popcorn. Neither one of them had felt like going to bed and there was a good late movie on. "I wish there was something we could do."

"If I could just clear him once and for all," Nancy said.

"Well, forget about it for a while. Maybe it'll sort itself out." She fiddled with the dial until she got the right channel. "Nancy, there's something I've got to tell you."

"You saw something on the airplane?" Nancy was instantly alert.

"Boy, did I!"

"Something Linda Cotilla did?"

"Not Linda—Mark."

It took Nancy a second to make the connection. "Mark, the copilot?"

Bess closed her eyes and sank against the cushions of the couch. "I think I'm in love," she said, her breath escaping in a sigh.

"You're always in love. What did this Mark do?"

" 'This Mark' didn't *do* anything. Get your mind off the mystery for a few minutes. He just bought me lunch at a great restaurant not too far from the L.A. airport and told me he hoped I was staying on the same route for a while."

Nancy had to grin. No matter where they went or what they did, Bess always seemed to find the perfect guy.

"I guess I'd better forget the movie and turn in if I'm going to make it through another day," Bess said.

"Yeah, me, too. I've got to talk to Blake Maxell tomorrow, and I'm not looking forward to it."

"What's the matter with Maxell?"

Nancy snorted. "He's suffering from grouchitis. He really went overboard yelling at one of the ticket agents today." Nancy described the scene between Maxell and Celia.

"That's nothing. Linda Cotilla makes Maxell look like a saint," Bess said as she unrolled her sleeping bag. She and Nancy flipped a coin for the couch, and Nancy won. "Story of my life," Bess grumbled.

"Now wait a minute. You got the couch last night, and you said things were going great with you and Mark."

"That's true." Bess snuggled inside her bag up to her chin. "Wait until you meet him, Nancy. He's a dream come true."

Long after Bess had gone to sleep, Nancy lay awake and hoped Jennifer and Sean's relationship hadn't become a nightmare.

The airport was bustling early the next afternoon. There were so many weekend travelers that Nancy had to weave her way through crowds and luggage just to get past Victory's main counter to the door to the offices.

"I've got to see Blake Maxell," she said to herself. She was just about to go inside when Preston Talbot and Blake Maxell exited through the door.

"Oh, Nancy," Mr. Talbot said distractedly, "this is Blake Maxell, our district manager. I was just telling him about you and your investigation."

"Pleased to meet you, Ms. Drew," Blake said. "Preston and I were just going to have a lunch meeting about this supposed smuggling ring," he added coolly. "Why don't you join us?"

"Great," Nancy agreed. She wished he'd thaw out a little. But this was a perfect opportunity to pick Maxell's brain, and she wasn't going to be put off by his manner.

The lunch meeting was to be in the airport's most luxurious restaurant. In her casual clothes, Nancy felt out of place, but she swallowed her misgivings and preceded the men into the dimly lit restaurant.

The hostess seated them at a corner table with a view of the northeast runway. Beyond the runway, they could see the gray-green waters of Puget Sound glimmering in the afternoon sun.

"I've told Blake all about your investigation so far," Mr. Talbot said to Nancy.

"That's right—and frankly, I think your theories are a little farfetched, Ms. Drew." Blake Maxell barely even glanced at her as he spoke. He reached for the menu and scanned it. "It's just not plausible," Maxell went on, still eyeing the menu. "How would anybody pull it off?"

"I was hoping you could help me on that," Nancy said diffidently. "Mr. Talbot said you would know better than he does about who could possibly run a smuggling ring and get away with it."

For the first time Maxell's gaze met hers. A faint smile touched his lips. *"I* would?"

"You're more involved with personnel," Nancy said, trying to keep the anger out of her voice. "And more involved with operations."

"Ms. Drew—" He folded his menu and looked directly at her. "It sounds to me as if you're letting this idea of being a girl detective go to your head. Jennifer Bishop is a friend of yours, isn't she?"

"Yes," Nancy said shortly.

"And she's the one who called you in?"

Nancy nodded.

"Do you really think she's qualified to decide whether there's trouble at Victory Airlines?"

"Jennifer's not the kind of person to make up stories," Nancy said as calmly as she could.

"Ah." He sat back as if she'd revealed something damaging—but as far as Nancy could tell, she hadn't backed down at all. For some reason she found herself turning to Preston Talbot for help.

Mr. Talbot cleared his throat. "I would like to believe you're right, Blake," he said. "But there is the matter of the note."

"What note?"

Talbot explained about the rock being thrown through his window.

"That's preposterous!" Maxell said when Mr. Talbot had finished. "Why would anyone want to threaten you, Ms. Drew?"

"Maybe they were worried I might get too close to the truth," Nancy suggested.

Maxell's expression showed how ludicrous he thought that was.

The waitress came and asked for their order. Maxell ordered one of the most expensive items on the menu, and Talbot, after much deliberation, ordered the same. Nancy just asked for a bowl of soup and a salad. She was worried she couldn't afford the meal.

While they were being served, Maxell seemed to change his attitude somewhat. "If what you say is true," he began, making it clear he still thought it highly possible Nancy was exaggerating, "then we need to beef up security until we get to the bottom of this thing."

"Good idea. How do you want to do it?" Mr. Talbot asked.

"I'll check with Dawkins in customs. I'll have him go through every item in every bag and crate that comes into this country. Also, Grant Sweeney should personally check the unloading of the planes. I don't want anything to fall through the cracks."

"I—uh—I wouldn't recommend Sweeney," Nancy put in.

"Why not?" Blake Maxell asked suspiciously.

"I think he might be involved in the smuggling."

"Well, Sweeney's the only man I completely trust," Maxell answered.

Although Grant Sweeney would hardly have been her choice, he *was* the man in charge of baggage. And Maxell had every reason to trust him.

Just then the check arrived. "I'll get it," Blake said, snatching the tab away from Nancy when she tried to see how much she owed. "This one's on Victory."

As they walked out, Nancy said to Maxell, "Do you think I could have a list of employees who could run a smuggling scam without raising suspicions?"

"I'll see what I can do, Ms. Drew. But let me make one thing clear: no matter what's going on around here, I don't want you here. If Preston wants you, fine. Stay on. But if it were up to me, the whole affair would be handled internally and then the police would be called in." His smile was faint. "I don't have a lot of faith in amateur detectives."

He turned and left. Nancy hardly knew what to say. Even Preston Talbot seemed embarrassed.

"Blake's a man of action," he said, apologizing. "He's never learned the fine art of finesse. That's why I handle the press."

And it's a good thing, too, Nancy thought, or Victory's reputation would go right down the tubes.

"I'd better get back to work," she said.

"Keep me posted," Talbot answered, waving as he walked away.

For a moment Nancy just stood in the center of the terminal. She was furious. Maxell had been rude and overbearing. And he'd been cruelly honest about what he thought of her abilities. She would have to prove herself to him!

Nancy took the stairs down to the lower level, intending to confront Grant Sweeney once and for all. If she could get some kind of confession out of him, maybe then Maxell would have to acknowledge her worth!

She learned that Sweeney was outside, loading a plane destined for the Orient. Her pulse quickening, Nancy wondered if it was a 747.

Quickly she ducked out the metal doorway and onto the tarmac. The huge silver plane was parked at the gate. The door to the baggage compartment was open, the portable stairway parked alongside.

Grant was just closing the plane's baggage compartment door when Nancy appeared at the bottom of the stairway. She waved at him, and Grant stood still for a moment. Then his face turned dark red, and he charged down the steps straight for her!

Chapter

Eleven

NANCY TOOK A step backward as Grant charged toward her. She held up her hands to ward him off—but instead of attacking her, he simply swept past her, bumping into her and knocking her off balance. Scrambling to her feet, Nancy chased after him.

"I want to talk to you!" she screamed above the noise of a departing plane.

Sweeney ignored her. He strode rapidly toward the building. Nancy ran after him, but she was stopped for a minute by a loading truck.

She followed Grant inside and just caught a glimpse of him disappearing at the back of the building. As Nancy dashed after him, Paul stepped in front of her.

"Hello, beautiful," he said with a friendly grin. "Look, let's forget about Sean. I know this great little intimate restaurant where we could have dinner. . . ."

"Sorry, Paul. I don't have the time." She tried to get past him, but he blocked her again. "What are you doing?" she demanded.

"Trying to get your attention." His smile was innocent.

By the time Nancy could get past him, Sweeney was long gone. She ran to his office, but the door was locked—and when she pounded on it, no one answered.

Did that mean he was gone or just playing possum as he had the last time she knocked on his door?

She turned back to walk to the baggage room and thought about the way Paul had deliberately cut her off. What had he been trying to do?

Absentmindedly Nancy wandered back into the baggage room and over to the window, her eyes on the plane Grant Sweeney had just finished loading. It was just backing away from the gate. Watching it Nancy wondered about its destination.

As it started forward and picked up speed, Nancy's thoughts returned to Grant Sweeney. He was dangerous—and he seemed to be running scared. He looked so guilty when she had caught him loading the plane. What exactly was he up to?

Suddenly Nancy's pulse leapt. She'd been so lost in thought that she hadn't paid much attention to what type of plane he'd been loading. Could it have been a 747?

She hurried over to two baggage handlers. They were Paul and Sean. "Was that a seven forty-seven that just left?" Nancy asked. "It looked like it."

Sean didn't say anything—just tightened his lips and turned aside. Nancy had to repeat the question to Paul.

"The flight we just loaded? Nah, that was a DC ten. Seven forty-sevens have an upper seating level. You can always tell by the two rows of windows. But a DC ten's as big as a seven forty-seven."

"Thanks. Is there any special way you load these planes? I mean, do you have specific ones to load?"

Sean threw several canvas bags on top of a mountainous pile in the trailer. "Come on, Nancy. What do you really want to know?" he asked.

"I was just curious."

"Sure you were." His tone was scathing. "You're trying to pin this smuggling thing on us!"

"*What?*" Paul was incredulous. "What smuggling thing?"

Nancy could have strangled Sean. "Nothing that I can really talk about," she said.

97

"Is that why you're hanging around here all the time? You want to prove one of us is smuggling?" Paul looked disgusted. "Well, forget it. You can just nose your way right out of here. Grant was right about you."

"What did Grant say about me?" she asked quickly.

"He said that you were trouble and to keep you away from him."

"Is that why you stopped me from chasing him?" Nancy asked.

Paul nodded almost sheepishly.

Sean finally looked at her and walked over to her. He put his arms on her shoulders and stared into her eyes. Nancy could see how unhappy he was, but he appeared to be determined. "Look, Nancy, I know you're just doing your job. But think about Paul and me for a moment, okay? Grant Sweeney's our boss. This job means everything to us. We don't want to jeopardize it."

"That's right," Paul said emphatically. "Whatever you're doing, just stay away from me."

"But isn't Preston Talbot your boss, too?" Nancy asked. "*He's* given me the okay. Why can't you?"

"Because Jennifer coerced Talbot into having you help. How could he say no when you were already on your way out here? Please, Nancy, just back off."

Nancy turned on her heel and left without

another word. How could she prove to them that she needed them to help her?

Nancy checked her watch. Sean and Paul would be getting off work soon, and Bess and Jennifer's flight should be back. Thinking she might just as well wait for them at the apartment, she headed for the stairs.

Halfway there Nancy heard sharp staccato footsteps coming her way. Then a flight attendant with blunt-cut shoulder-length blond hair suddenly rounded the corner and ran straight into her.

"Oh, sorry," Nancy apologized, though it really wasn't her fault. In that brief second she read the woman's nameplate: "Linda Cotilla, Senior Flight Attendant."

"My fault," Linda answered shortly. She swept past Nancy without a glance.

Nancy hesitated only a moment. Then she ducked around the corner and started following Linda.

Linda kept right on going. Glad she had on soft-soled flats, Nancy walked quietly behind Linda. Nancy's heart began to pound. Linda was heading straight for Grant Sweeney's office!

Nancy held her breath as she heard Linda's knuckles rap quietly on the door.

To her surprise she heard a man's muffled voice answer.

"It's me," Linda said urgently. "Hurry up! I've got to talk to you!"

Nancy heard the latch click back. Then Sweeney said, "Are you crazy? What are you doing down here? Don't you know that girl's around?"

"She's not the only one. There's another," Linda said anxiously. "Her name's Bess Marvin, and she's masquerading as a flight attendant. I heard it from Talbot. She's on my flight. I think she knows about the smuggling!"

"Shut up and get in here!" Sweeney growled. The door slammed shut.

With her back against the wall, Nancy slowly worked her way to Sweeney's door. She could hear faint voices from within. Leaning closer to the door, she pressed her ear against the panel.

"They're on to us," Linda was saying, her voice rising hysterically. "It's only a matter of time before it all comes down, and who do you think's going to take the blame? *We are!* We're the ones who'll be thrown to the wolves—and guess who'll get away scot-free?"

"Shut up! You want someone to hear you? Like that Drew girl?"

"I don't care! I'm scared to death. Just—"

Nancy didn't get a chance to hear any more. A hand suddenly clapped over her mouth, and strong arms started dragging her down the hall.

Chapter

Twelve

NANCY STRUGGLED WILDLY against her captor's grip, but she couldn't get away. He pulled her down the hallway around the corner, and when they were out of earshot of Grant's door, he hissed, "Just what do you think you're doing?"

Nancy went limp with relief. "Sean!" she murmured against his hand.

Sean took his hand from her mouth, and Nancy twisted from his grasp. "What am *I* doing?" she demanded, her fear giving way to anger. "What are *you* doing? Trying to keep me from solving this mystery, or are you involved in this smuggling operation somehow?" she asked.

Sean's jaw sagged. "Do you really think I am?"

"I don't know!"

"Well, I'm not," he said flatly. "But I guess you're going to have to figure that out on your own." Glancing over her shoulder, he asked, "What would you have done if Grant had come out of his office and caught you eavesdropping?"

"Well, it wouldn't have been the first time!" Nancy snapped.

"What's that supposed to mean?"

"It means he practically bashed my head in with a wrench the last time I went to his office. If you hadn't yanked me away just then, I might have learned something important. Linda Cotilla's in with Grant right now!"

"Linda Cotilla!"

"That's right. She was saying something about smuggling and how Bess and I were on to them. Look, I'll explain later."

Nancy left Sean standing in the hallway and ran back to Grant's office. But she could hear two pairs of footsteps retreating in the distance, and when she listened at the door, the room sounded ominously quiet. "I could scream," Nancy muttered in frustration. "They've already left."

A very subdued Sean appeared at her elbow. Swallowing hard, he said, "I've been thinking, maybe I owe you an apology."

"Oh, yes?" Nancy didn't feel very forgiving.

"I was mad because you dragged Jennifer into

this, and now I've messed things up for you. I wanted to be your friend, Nancy. But I had a talk with Mr. Talbot and—"

Nancy's eyes searched Sean's. "Mr. Talbot was the one who turned you against me?"

"He didn't actually turn me against you. He's just worried about Victory's reputation. And when he thought about what would happen to it if something happened to you and Jennifer—" Sean shrugged.

Nancy leaned against the wall. "Didn't it ever occur to you that he was trying to put a wedge between us?"

"Mr. Talbot?" Sean said in disbelief.

"If he's behind the smuggling ring, then it would be to his advantage to keep you from siding with me."

Sean managed a harsh laugh. "I don't believe any of this."

"Believe it," Nancy said. "Talbot and Sweeney are probably working together—and they mean business." It was such a relief to be able to trust Sean again! Nancy felt as if a weight had been lifted from her shoulders.

Sean exhaled heavily. "If Talbot's really the man behind the smuggling ring, it makes me sick. This whole management training program was his idea. But what'll happen to the program if he's exposed?"

"I don't know." Nancy was genuinely sorry she

had thought the management trainee program had been the basis for bringing new recruits into the smuggling ring. Maybe Mr. Talbot had brought in Rod Fullerton, but other management trainees—like Sean, and probably Celia—were completely innocent. "If the management program has been successful, I don't see why the next person in charge won't keep it going," Nancy added.

Sean forced a weak smile. "Okay, enough feeling sorry for myself. How can I help?"

Glancing thoughtfully at Grant's door, Nancy said, "We've got to prove Talbot's in on this, and we need to find how customs is being bypassed and what kind of contraband is being brought in."

"Whew. You don't ask for much, do you?"

"That's what it's going to take to get to the bottom of this," Nancy said grimly. "Are you with me?"

"All the way," Sean agreed, his blue eyes telling her again how sorry he was. "You want to search the planes when they come in?"

"No, I can't search all the planes," Nancy said, feeling frustrated. "I thought the smugglers were just using seven forty-sevens, but now I don't know . . ." Her voice trailed off as her mind spun ahead. "Celia gave me a ton of printouts. Maybe the answers are in those sheets."

Checking his watch, Sean said, "Look, I just have to go back and punch out." He glanced at Nancy. "If you'd like some help, you and I could head back to Jennifer's apartment and go through the printouts together."

"Terrific!" Nancy said.

"This is no use," Nancy said back in Jennifer's apartment. She got up from her chair and stretched. "We could go over these all day and all night and still not come up with anything!"

"There must be something special in here about a seven forty-seven," Sean said, shaking his head.

Nancy turned to stare at Sean, her mind racing. "Talk about not being able to see the forest for the trees," she said. "That's the problem! We just assumed seven forty-seven referred to the airplane type."

Sean looked at her as if she were crazy.

"What if it isn't a plane at all? What if seven forty-seven stands for a flight number or something?"

It was Sean's turn to stare. "That plane that Grant loaded this afternoon," he said slowly. "It was a DC ten, but what was its flight number?"

Nancy shuffled through the printouts on the table and scanned the list of DC 10s, but none of them had the flight number 747.

"I was wrong," she said, disappointed. Then her eye caught something else—and a chill slid up her spine. "Oh, Sean!" she said, hardly daring to believe her eyes.

"What?"

"That flight, the one that Grant was loading? It got into Seattle airport this morning at seven forty-seven!"

"Let me see that!" Sean said.

He looked over her shoulder, reading down the list. "And it came from Malaysia," he said. "Do you suppose something was on that flight?"

"The plane had already been unloaded. I bet Grant was just making sure all the contraband was out of it. When I showed up, he panicked." Nancy paced around the kitchen. "And you know what else I think? I think that seven forty-seven is how they tag flights for smuggling."

"How do you mean?"

"Suppose it's a code. It's how the smugglers know which flight to use to ship their goods. That number could be anything: plane type, departure or arrival time, maybe even flight number!"

"I think you've cracked the code, Nancy! You've done it!" Sean exclaimed.

In his exuberance, he caught her up in a big bear hug. "Now you can blow this investigation wide open. Wait till I tell Jennifer!"

Suddenly the front door slammed shut. Nancy and Sean looked around to see Jennifer and Bess come into the kitchen.

"Wait until you tell Jennifer what?" Jennifer asked in a brittle voice as she stared at the two of them.

Chapter

Thirteen

"JENNIFER!" SEAN SAID, dropping his arms from around Nancy.

Jennifer just stared at him, the color leaving her face. "Don't mind me," she said in a flat, trembling voice. "Go right ahead with what you were doing. It's a free country." She twisted around and started walking stiffly toward the bedroom.

"Jennifer!" Sean called, walking after her. But she slammed the door in his face.

Bess's brows were sky-high. "Well," she said, sinking into one of the kitchen chairs.

"This is too much." Nancy was divided between disbelief and frustration. "You're not going to tell me you think Sean and I are interested in each other, are you?"

Bess shook her head. "I know you better than that, Nancy. But it was a terrible day. Linda Cotilla was even worse than before. And then Jen and I had to stay late and do paperwork." She gave Nancy and Sean a crooked smile. "I think seeing you two together was kind of the last straw."

"I'll talk to her," Sean said, starting for Jennifer's room. "I owe her an apology for the other night anyway."

"Guess what? We think we've figured out what seven forty-seven means," Nancy said to Bess.

"You mean it's not the airplane?"

As Nancy started to tell Bess about their findings, Jennifer came back into the room. It was obvious that she'd been crying, but she tried to pretend nothing was wrong.

Nancy couldn't bear to have her friend think she had been trying to steal Sean. "Hey, Jen," she said. "Sean came here to see you. You know that."

Jennifer didn't answer. Sean stepped closer to her. "Come on, Jen," he said in a low voice. "Let's get out of here so we can talk. I'm sorry about the other night. Nancy and I had a talk today, and I realized a few things about you and me, too."

Jennifer didn't seem to know what to do, but

when Sean steered her toward the door, she made no protest.

"I hope they get things worked out," Bess said.

"Me, too. I wish I could convince Jennifer that Ned's the only guy I'm interested in."

"Maybe Sean'll convince her," Bess said with a smile. "So what's the deal with him, anyway? Why is he off the suspect list?"

"He was so destroyed by what I told him that I knew he wasn't involved. He doesn't want to believe Mr. Talbot is behind all this, but it's hard not to suspect him."

Bess kicked off her shoes, moaned, and rubbed her feet. "Well, I'm glad Sean's on our side. I just wish I could get Linda Cotilla off my back. The woman is an absolute witch!"

"Hold on to your socks, Bess—Linda's involved in the smuggling ring, too."

"What? You're kidding!"

Nancy repeated what she'd overheard of the conversation between Grant and Linda. "I'd like to find out what she's up to," Nancy finished. "I think I'll book a seat on your flight tomorrow and see for myself. I'll have to wear a disguise, though. You've got a ton of clothes, Bess. Let me wear that black sweater-and-skirt outfit you brought. Then I'll have to figure out something to do with my hair."

"My black sweater and skirt? You'll swim in them!" Bess declared. Then she caught herself. "Oh, I get it. That's the idea."

"But what'll I do about this hair?"

"I think I've got the answer for you," Bess said, grinning. "Linda will never recognize you! Just give me the keys to the car."

"Bess—" Nancy said.

Then the door opened, and Jennifer and Sean came back inside. From the expressions on their faces it was clear they'd worked out their problems.

"Sorry, Nancy," Jennifer said, darting her an apologetic glance. "I was just upset. I overreacted."

"It's already forgotten," Nancy assured her. "I'm just glad we're all on the same side again. Now we can get down to business."

"Speaking of business, Jennifer," Bess said, "how would you and Sean like to do a little shopping with me? I've got to pick up a few things for Nancy."

"What kind of things?" Jennifer asked, following Bess to the door.

"You'll see," she answered mysteriously, and the three of them left together.

A few minutes after they'd gone, Miranda came in looking totally worn out. "That's my last flight for a few days," she said. "I'm going to go to bed and sleep for a week!" She said good night and staggered off to her room.

To occupy her time, Nancy made a list of all inbound Victory flights that met the 747 code requirements. She was just finishing up when

Bess, Jennifer, and Sean returned. Bess was holding a large brown paper bag.

"Bess has got the perfect disguise for you," Jennifer said enthusiastically.

"I can hardly wait," Nancy answered dryly.

Bess began pulling all kinds of things from the sack: costume jewelry, a black lace headband with a huge bow, a pair of black stockings, and a can of some kind of spray that she instantly began to shake.

"What is *that*?" Nancy eyed the can suspiciously.

"Your new hair color."

"Oh, no!" Nancy backed away. "I'm not dying my hair. No way!"

"It's glitter spray. It'll artificially darken your hair and fill it full of gold glitter. You can wash it out when you get home tomorrow."

"Are you crazy? I'll look as though I'm auditioning for a rock video!"

"Well, you won't look like *you*. You can wear dark glasses," Bess said, holding up her hands when Nancy started to protest further. "Look, you're the detective, right? Well, I'm the fashion expert. This time you listen to me."

It was still dark outside when Nancy, Bess, and Jennifer had gotten up to create the "new" Nancy Drew.

"There," Bess said. Nancy uncovered her eyes to see the result. Her hair waved to her shoulders in a bushy curtain. The spray had darkened it to an auburn shade and spangled it with flecks of gold.

Bess pulled the headband on next and tilted the black lace bow jauntily to one side.

"What do you think?" Bess asked as Nancy examined herself critically.

"Let's see," Nancy said, turning around. Bess's black sweater practically swallowed her up. Long gold earrings dangled from her ears, and a heavy V-shaped choker encircled her throat.

Striking a pose, Nancy said, "Coffee, tea, or—"

"Murder," Jennifer broke in, coming from the living room. Her face was white. In her hand was a newspaper. She thrust it in front of Nancy's nose. "Look! The brakes on Rod Fullerton's car gave out!"

"*What?*" Nancy grabbed the newspaper and skimmed the article. The police had investigated the fatal accident that had taken Rod Fullerton's life and had linked it to faulty brakes.

"Read it on the plane!" Bess said, handing Nancy her dark glasses. "We've got to get going. Now."

Rather than risk detection by using her pass to board the plane, Nancy bought a ticket under the name Ms. N. Nickerson. Wait until Ned hears about this! she thought with a laugh.

People kept staring at her as she walked along. Nancy glanced into one of the mirrors beside the airport's Vapor Trail Café. With scarlet lipstick, red heels, black nylons, the oversize black sweater and skirt, and her wild new hair, Nancy's own father wouldn't have recognized her!

Nancy checked in and boarded the plane. She threw her overnight bag with a change of clothes into an overhead storage bin. She planned to take a different flight back to Seattle—and she couldn't wait to get into her comfortable black cords and flats in Los Angeles.

Nancy looked for Linda Cotilla, but she didn't see her. She decided the flight attendant must be in the back galley.

Nancy's aisle seat was about halfway down the coach section of the 727. The 727 was much smaller than the 747s, but it was roomy, anyway. The chair beside her was empty, but the window seat was occupied by a businessman. He looked her over from head to toe, then snapped open his newspaper in silent disapproval.

Amused, Nancy picked up a magazine and began leafing through it. When all the passengers had been seated, Linda came out of the back galley, walked to the front of the plane, and picked up the microphone.

"Ladies and gentlemen, welcome to flight two thirty-three, nonstop to Los Angeles. We will be departing in about five minutes. Please make sure your seats and tray tables are in an upright position and fasten your seat belts for takeoff."

Settling into the seat, Nancy heaved a sigh of contentment. She had wanted to take a trip somewhere. A day flight to Los Angeles and back was better than nothing. She was going to get her chance to meet Bess's Mark, too, when the flight landed.

Linda walked slowly down the aisle to check everyone's seat, and suddenly stopped right in front of Nancy.

"You!" Linda exclaimed angrily. "What are *you* doing on this flight?"

Chapter

Fourteen

So the jig was up. Nancy slowly lifted her eyes, meeting Linda's furious stare. But Linda's gaze was focused past Nancy's head on the person seated behind her.

"Hi, Linda," a male voice said easily. "Something wrong with my taking a flight to L.A.?"

Linda drew a deep breath, said, "Of course not," and attempted a smile. But Nancy saw the way she strode toward the galley, her steps jerky and agitated.

Nancy pretended to drop her magazine in the aisle. When she bent to pick it up, she twisted slightly and glanced backward. The man in the seat behind her was no one she had ever seen before.

Who was he? Another member of the smuggling gang?

Once in the air Nancy observed Linda. Twice she dropped a passenger's cup, and when she served breakfast trays, her hands were so unsteady that the trays shook. If Linda hadn't been the senior flight attendant, she would certainly have been fired, Nancy thought.

In the Los Angeles airport Nancy met Bess and Jennifer at Victory's Mile High Room, a private room for employees of the airline and special frequent flyers.

"I saw Linda head in another direction, so we're safe in here," Jennifer said. "Come on, Nancy. There's a restroom where you can change—it even has a shower."

After washing and drying her hair, she changed out of Bess's clothes and pulled on her own.

Feeling more like herself in the black cords and turquoise shirt, she rejoined the others and was introduced to a young man dressed in a black Victory uniform.

"This is Mark," Bess said with a proud smile.

Mark pulled out a chair for Nancy. "What a transformation!" he said. "I saw you when you got on the plane."

For some reason Nancy blushed. "I was—er—working undercover."

Mark's mouth twitched. Nancy was glad to see

he had a sense of humor. "Bess said you were a detective."

"That's right. In fact, that's why I called her to come to Seattle," Jennifer put in. "Nancy's the best."

"Tell me all about you and Victory Airlines," Nancy said encouragingly to Mark, hoping to get a fresh perspective on the case.

Mark was more than happy to tell her about his job and how he'd come to work for Victory. While he talked, Bess watched him with adoring eyes.

"Has either of you ever been in any kind of danger in the air?" Nancy asked Jennifer and Mark.

Jennifer shook her head, but Mark nodded. "Once," he admitted. "We were flying through some really tough weather, and the hydraulic line to the rudder snapped. We lost pressure to the wings and brakes and had to make a flaps-up landing."

"Flaps-up landing?" It sounded bad.

"Normally, when a plane approaches the runway to land, the pilot lowers the flaps on the wings. The flaps add drag and slow the plane down. As soon as the wheels hit the runway, the brakes are applied, and the plane gradually comes to a stop.

"In a flaps-up landing, with no brakes, the plane approaches the runway *fast*. As soon as the wheels come down and the plane lands, you just have to ride with it until it comes to a stop on its own."

"What if you run out of runway?" Nancy asked.

Mark smiled. "That's the problem. There aren't many runways long enough to make that kind of landing. When the plane runs out of landing strip, it just keeps heading forward across a field or asphalt to whatever's in front of it. You'd just better hope there's nothing there."

"Like other planes," Nancy said.

"Or buildings."

"Does Puget Sound Airport have a runway long enough to handle that kind of emergency landing?" Bess asked, the possibilities widening her eyes.

"The northeast runway is five thousand feet long. It's the longest one we've got."

Nancy recalled that that was the runway she had seen from the window of the restaurant Preston Talbot and Blake Maxell had taken her to. It was also the runway used for most of the jumbo jets.

The talk turned more general as they ate lunch in the Mile High Room. After dessert Mark, Jennifer, and Bess went back to the plane. Nancy's flight took off a little later than the Victory flight. As she flew back to Seattle, Nancy went over the case in her mind and decided she'd like to talk to Linda alone.

Back in Seattle, near Victory's counter, Nancy looked for Bess and Jennifer. But the first person she saw was Linda Cotilla. And Linda was in a furious conversation with Grant Sweeney!

Nancy ducked behind a pillar and tried to move closer to where Linda and Grant were standing.

As soon as she got within earshot, though, Grant suddenly stalked off. Linda stood still for several moments, then walked away in the other direction.

What's going on? Nancy wondered. Did they see me?

As surreptitiously as possible she started after Linda, following her to the Vapor Trail Café. When Linda took a seat at a quiet table in the corner, Nancy slipped inside and stood in a sheltered spot by the counter. She wasn't really surprised when Grant Sweeney strolled in and sat down in the seat across from Linda.

Nancy looked around. There was a half wall dividing the café into two sections. Vertical blinds ran from the top rail to the ceiling. Linda and Grant were on one side of the wall, and the table that backed up to them on the near side was empty. Casually Nancy walked to the table, slipped into the chair, and scooted it as far back as possible, hoping to hear their conversation.

She leaned toward the wall. Her heart began to pound when she heard Grant's deep voice.

"It's too risky to be seen together like this," he was saying.

Linda spoke so low Nancy could hardly catch anything she said. Then Linda said something about "seven forty-seven." Nancy sat bolt upright in her chair.

Grant Sweeney actually laughed. "Yeah, well, he thinks of everything."

Nancy strained to hear Linda's soft voice. She could only make out some of the words. "I want out! I saw Daw . . . on the plane. Don't think . . . know what that means! I . . . go on much longer."

"You should have thought of that earlier," Grant said without sympathy. "You know what the man upstairs does to deserters."

Linda's voice was completely indistinguishable after that. Nancy thought she might even be crying.

But Grant's voice came out cold and chilling. "Better be careful, or the boss'll take care of you, too. You'll end up at the bottom of a cliff just like Rod!"

Nancy sat transfixed, her hands gripping the edge of the table in front of her. Proof that Rod had been murdered!

Then Nancy heard chairs scrape back. She searched around desperately for an escape. If they see me now I'm done for! she thought.

Seconds later Linda walked out. Grant stood near the doorway. He seemed in no big hurry to leave.

If he looks back and spots me . . . Nancy agonized, turning her shoulder his way.

She nearly jumped out of her skin when a shadow fell across her table. "What are you doing in here?" Paul asked.

Nancy glanced up. Grant Sweeney was starting to turn her way.

Impulsively, Nancy threw her arms around Paul and gave him a big kiss. Several long seconds passed before Nancy dared to shoot a glance over Paul's shoulder. But when she did, Grant was gone.

"Whew. That was close! Thanks for covering for me," Nancy said, picking up her purse.

Paul was looking at her in total bemusement. He blinked rapidly several times. For once in his life he seemed to have absolutely nothing to say.

"Look, I've got to go," Nancy said hurriedly. "I'll—I'll explain later. And thanks again."

"Does this mean you might accept my offer of a date?" he asked, but Nancy just smiled as she sidled past him and out of the restaurant.

She practically ran to the main terminal. Rod Fullerton definitely had been murdered! It was something to tell the police! Nancy tried to decide whom to see first: Jennifer and Bess, Sean, or Preston Talbot.

"You know what the man upstairs does to deserters."

Grant's words hit Nancy like a thunderbolt. The man upstairs. *Preston Talbot!* Talbot's office was on the sixth floor. Victory's offices only went as high as the seventh. The man upstairs couldn't be anyone else!

She turned blindly toward Victory's counter. Celia was waving frantically for her to come over.

"I have a message Jennifer Bishop asked me to pass along to you."

"A message?"

"Apparently a flu bug's going around, and half the flight attendants are down with it. Jennifer and Bess have to work a late flight with a layover. They won't be back until late tomorrow. The flight leaves in a few hours, so you'll have time to catch them if you want."

Nancy snapped back to attention. "They have to work another flight?" she asked in disbelief.

Celia nodded. "Sometimes it happens when we're understaffed. Most of the time the flight attendants love it—they get paid time and a half. But I thought Jennifer and Bess looked pretty tired."

Nancy asked, "Do you know who put them on that flight? Who arranged for them to fly out?"

"Blake Maxell, I suppose. He's in charge of operations."

Nancy felt marginally better. She had had a bad feeling about their change of schedule, but as long as Preston Talbot wasn't involved, she couldn't see how it would matter.

Not wanting to worry Bess and Jennifer, Nancy decided to see if Sean was still around. Though his shift was over, he sometimes stayed later.

She wound her way through the lower levels and opened the door to the baggage handling room. Grant Sweeney was inside putting on a slicker to go out into the soft drizzle.

Through the open doorway Nancy could see that a plane had just landed. The signal man was waving his scarlet beacons, bringing the plane to one of the nearest gates.

As Grant started walking back toward her, Nancy ducked out of sight behind the door. He rattled open the second huge metal door to the outdoors, then jumped into one of the truck and trailer rigs and headed outside.

One of the other baggage handlers appeared, also dressed in a slicker, and started running after him. "What are you doing?" he called to Grant. "I thought I was supposed to unload seven four seven."

"We can unload it together!" Grant hollered back. "If we're not finished up by the time the next flight comes in, you can start on that one while I finish this one." Both men left.

Seven four seven. Nancy's heart thumped unevenly. This was it! One of the flights used by the smugglers—and Grant Sweeney wanted to unload it!

I have to check that plane! she thought.

Looking around, Nancy saw several more slickers lined up near the back door. She raced over and snatched one off the rack. Quickly she pulled the black rubber cloak around her and over her head.

She walked into the rain, hugging the building as she moved around the corner to where Grant and the other handler were unloading flight 747.

Under a darkened eave Nancy waited until both carts had been filled and the two men were driving their vehicles back to the loading area.

Now was her chance!

Nancy darted toward the plane and up the stairway. Although Grant and the other man would be occupied for a while unloading the cargo, she'd be pressing her luck to stay inside more than a few minutes.

"Of course there's always the possibility that Grant unloaded the smuggled goods first," Nancy muttered to herself. "No, not with the other handler there."

Nancy searched anxiously, hoping for some clue. There were still so many packages and so much luggage! Minutes passed, and her search was fruitless.

She heard the baggage trucks coming back and glanced out the doorway. There was no time to escape. If they saw her on the portable stairway, she'd be a sitting duck.

Nancy backed away from the door into a dark corner of the compartment. She heard the men's footsteps on the stairway. What if they found her? Could she bluff her way out? What would Grant do?

"Okay, let's get this big stuff out of here first," Grant said. "Start over here."

They were near the door. Nancy sank down, accidentally knocking over a very small crate to her right—it started toppling toward her. She caught it silently, closing her eyes in relief.

Carefully she lowered the crate to the floor. She hardly glanced at it. But at the last minute something caught her attention.

Its point of origin was listed as Singapore. Nothing unusual in that, but as Nancy peered more closely she saw something written on one corner.

Her heart somersaulted. Written clearly in tiny numbers was the smugglers' identifying mark: 747.

Chapter

Fifteen

NANCY WAITED UNTIL the two men had finished loading up their trailers again and the sound of the trucks' engines had faded. Luckily one of the boards on the crate was loose and Nancy could pry it up.

Beneath the strawlike packing were several beautiful jade figurines. She dug deeper—and lifted out a Chinese vase!

It was nearly a twin to the one Rod had given Miranda. The scene was slightly different, but the colors were the same. Nancy was sure it was genuine Ming.

Quickly she gathered up the crate. She hurried

toward the door, peeked out, and climbed down the stairway.

Now, where to go next? Nancy knew she couldn't be caught with the stolen goods. She pressed herself against the wall and waited around the corner until Grant and the other baggage handler went back to unloading the plane.

Glancing inside the baggage handling room, Nancy saw that several more handlers had returned and were loading luggage. As nonchalantly as possible, she pulled the hooded slicker closer around her face and walked briskly across the room. What if one of the handlers called out to her?

But none of them did. She got to the other side of the room near the stairway without a problem. Shedding the slicker, she balanced the wooden box on her hip and held it in place as she headed upstairs. She had proof!

With a start, Nancy realized that she had bypassed customs. But Grant Sweeney, or whoever else was involved, couldn't keep bringing boxes up from the baggage room without arousing suspicion. If the smuggling operation were as sophisticated as she suspected, there had to be another way.

Nancy raced up the last few steps, then opened the door to the outer terminal. She nearly dropped the crate when she heard someone call her name.

Sean was walking toward the door.

"I was just going downstairs to see if I could work an extra shift," he said. "Since Jennifer's on a flight, I thought I might as well work."

Nancy didn't waste any time with preliminaries. "Sean, you've got to help me," she said.

His eyes slowly drifted to the box in her hands. "What's that?" he asked.

"Evidence. Stolen merchandise, I'd bet. It came in on flight seven forty-seven and look—" She showed him the tiny numbers printed on the corner. "It's filled with jade figurines. There's even a vase like the one Rod gave Miranda."

"How did you get hold of it?"

"I'll tell you on the way to Talbot's office. I want to go straight up there and confront him with the evidence."

She was turning back for the elevator when Sean's hand closed around her arm. "Nancy, get serious," he said anxiously. "You can't just accuse him and throw this in his face. He'll do something drastic!"

Nancy knew that Sean was right. As she watched the elevator slowly descend to their floor, she said, "He needs to see me alone. If he believes I'm the only one who knows, he might feel he can do away with me and still be safe. He might even brag a little about his part in the smuggling ring."

"You're nuts," Sean muttered. "Nancy, he *can* do away with you, and he *will!*"

The elevator dinged, the doors slid open, and Blake Maxell brushed past them with hardly a glance.

"That's the answer!" Nancy said. "You go after Maxell and bring him to Talbot's office. Stay outside and listen to what's going on with me and Talbot. I'll make sure the door's left open a little. When Talbot starts talking, you guys rush in. I won't be in any real danger."

"I don't like it," Sean murmured, but when he saw how determined Nancy was, he turned to go after Maxell.

Nancy leapt into the elevator just as the doors started to close. Now, let Talbot be in his office, she thought grimly. This is no time to be chasing him all over the airport.

Outside the double doors to his office she took several deep breaths and knocked sharply, but all she heard was silence.

"He's got to be there," she said out loud. "He's got to!"

At the far end of the hall the elevator bell chimed and the doors slid open. Sean and Blake Maxell came quickly her way.

"He isn't there?" Sean asked, worried.

"I don't think so. At least he doesn't answer when I knock."

"What's this all about?" Maxell demanded, flicking back his sleeve to check his watch. "I'm on a tight schedule, you know."

With an effort Nancy held her temper. "We

believe Preston Talbot is the head of the smuggling ring. He's using Victory Airlines to bring in stolen merchandise," she said firmly.

Maxell only laughed. "Of all the ridiculous, slanderous accusations I've heard, this has got to be—"

"We have proof," Nancy cut him off shortly. She handed the box to Maxell. "If you take this to the police and ask them to check out the items inside, I'll bet my reputation as a detective they'll find out it's stolen merchandise."

Maxell's eyebrows drew together. "Where did you get this?" he demanded harshly.

"Off a flight that just came in from Singapore. Grant Sweeney's in on the ring. So is Linda Cotilla. Preston Talbot's the leader."

Maxell looked dazed. After several seconds of silence, he said in an entirely different tone of voice, "I may have been too hasty in my judgment of you, Ms. Drew." He pulled out his keys, fitted one into Talbot's lock, and opened the door.

The office was empty.

"Where could he be?" Nancy asked, pacing the plush surroundings.

"Maybe he's just gone home," Sean suggested. "It *is* late, you know."

Maxell walked over to the window, staring out into the dark night. "No, Preston's probably still here. I saw him not too long ago talking to Linda Cotilla," he said slowly.

"Did you hear any of their conversation?"

Blake turned away from the window, his expression sober and stern. "Linda mentioned the name Bess Marvin. And then Preston looked so odd. He headed down the concourse right afterward."

Nancy's blood ran cold. What were Linda and Talbot cooking up for Bess? "Sean," she asked, "do you know which flight Bess and Jennifer are on?"

"I think it's flight one ninety-one. It goes to Chicago and on to New York."

"I've got to talk to Bess," Nancy said. "I've got to make sure she's all right!"

"What do you want me to do?" Maxell asked, still holding the small crate. "I've got a small problem to deal with right now."

"Go," Nancy said. "And thanks. We'll check with you later." As soon as Maxell left, Nancy added, "We've got to find out if Linda Cotilla's on that flight with Bess and Jennifer!"

"You think she'll try something?" Sean asked, alarmed.

"I don't know. But I've got a bad feeling about it."

"Come on downstairs," said Sean. "We'll check the crew schedule with the gate agent."

They hurried to the end of the hall and raced down the stairs. Sean checked the monitor to see which gate Jennifer and Bess's flight departed from.

"Gate forty-three. They leave in five minutes."

"Quick. We've got to find out if Linda's on that

132

flight!" Nancy said, and Sean tersely told the ticketing agent to pull up the crew schedule on her computer terminal.

"The senior flight attendant is Linda Cotilla," the ticketing agent informed them.

Linda Cotilla! Nancy turned to Sean. "Go get Maxell. Tell him we've got trouble. I'm afraid Linda might try to hurt Jennifer and Bess."

"Okay." Sean had already turned on one foot.

"What's Maxell's office number in case I need you?" Nancy asked quickly.

"I don't know. It's on the seventh floor, I think."

"That's right," the ticketing agent spoke up, consulting her screen. "He just changed offices last year. Now he's in room seven forty-seven."

Chapter

Sixteen

NANCY COULDN'T BELIEVE her ears. "Room seven forty-seven?" she repeated.

"That's right."

"It's Maxell," Sean said. "Not Talbot. Maxell's behind the smuggling ring!"

Over their heads, they heard the disembodied voice announce, "Last call for flight one ninety-one to Chicago and on to New York."

"Sean, you've got to let the police know about Maxell," Nancy said. "He's got our evidence, and we just told him everything we know. It's only a matter of time before he comes after us. He may have already ordered Linda to do something to Bess and Jennifer!"

Sean's face was gray. "I'll go call them right now. What are you going to do?"

"Try to catch that flight!"

Nancy didn't waste any more time. She ran as fast as she could for the gate. The gate agent was just closing the doors as she arrived. Nancy grabbed his arm as he was shutting the door. "You've got to let me on board," Nancy pleaded. "Please! It's important."

"I'm sorry, miss—"

Nancy yanked out her pass. "Preston Talbot expects me to be on that plane," she said. "How will it look when I tell him one of his own agents was the reason I missed my flight?"

The gate agent opened his mouth to argue, then clamped it shut again, snapping up the hand-held intercom and speaking into it.

"They're holding the plane for you," he bit out. "Go on down."

"Thank you."

Linda Cotilla stood by the door as Nancy was admitted onto the plane. Linda's lips parted, and her face went white.

Nancy didn't say anything to her. And since she didn't have a ticket, she picked a seat near the rear of the plane, next to the galley. There was no one else seated near her.

"Nancy!" Bess exclaimed, rushing up to her. "What are you doing here?'

Nancy smiled grimly. "I had so much fun on my first flight, I thought I'd take another," she said.

Bess gave her a worried look. "I can't talk now—got to work. Fill me in later, okay?" she said. Then she went back to her duties.

Nancy watched out the window as the plane picked up speed. Its engines roared, and it suddenly lifted upward, leaving Seattle behind in a matter of minutes.

As soon as she could, Bess came back to Nancy. "What do you mean, you wanted to take another flight? Nancy, what's going on?"

"All I can tell you is I'm sure now that Rod Fullerton was murdered. Linda Cotilla knows."

"No!" Bess gasped.

"Shh! Listen, I got on this flight because I need to talk to her." She didn't add, *And make sure she doesn't harm you or Jennifer.*

Bess looked too shaken to ask more questions. She walked back to the galley without another word.

It had been Blake Maxell all along, Nancy saw that now. He'd been the man behind the smuggling ring, not Preston Talbot.

A snack was served on the flight, and shortly afterward the lights were dimmed and passengers settled in to sleep. Nancy just stayed where she was, waiting.

There were very few people on board. The rear of the plane where Nancy was sitting was practically empty.

In the aft galley Linda Cotilla was stacking empty trays back into their slots. Her concentration was so intense that she didn't notice when Nancy got up from her seat and leaned a shoulder against the galley doorway.

"Hello, Linda," Nancy said.

"Oh!" The tray she had been holding clattered to the floor. "Look what you made me do! Go back to your seat and leave me alone!"

"I need to talk to you."

"I'm busy," Linda hissed, glancing fearfully past Nancy as if she expected someone to materialize.

"I know you're trying to get out of the smuggling ring," Nancy said. "And I know you're scared to death."

Linda's lips quivered, but there was fire in her eyes. Her mouth tightened into a grim line.

"I'm here to break up the smuggling ring," Nancy tried again. "The one *you're* involved in."

"Get out of here and leave me alone!"

"I know about your connection to Grant Sweeney and Blake Maxell. I know that shipments of stolen merchandise are being brought in on flights somehow designated with the seven forty-seven code. And I know Rod Fullerton was murdered, and that you think you're next in line."

Linda stared at Nancy through wide, terrified eyes. For a moment Nancy thought she might break down completely. Then she managed to pull herself together. "It's too late," she whispered and turned away.

"It's not too late!" Nancy grabbed Linda by the

shoulders and forced her to meet her gaze. "I can help you."

"How?" There was resignation in Linda's voice, as if she had faced all the possibilities already and knew there was no hope left.

"If you tell me how you got into this thing, and who all the principal players are, I can do my best to get you a reduced sentence."

Linda leaned against the counter, wilting. "Oh, what's the use? He's going to kill me anyway."

"Maxell?" Nancy asked sharply.

"Yes. He'll kill you, too."

Nancy drew a deep breath. "We'll see about that. Now tell me how you got into this thing."

Linda sighed. "I wanted a promotion—and Blake Maxell was there, pushing all the right buttons. He told me he could guarantee I'd get everything I wanted if I'd just do a few simple things."

"What kind of things?"

"Smuggling. In the beginning he needed someone who was trusted and well-known with the customs agents to bring stuff through. All the guys knew me and liked me. They hardly ever searched my bags.

"But then the organization grew and Blake came up with the idea of the seven forty-seven code. He thought it was really clever. And then, when they got Dawkins involved . . ." Linda shuddered. "He's almost as bad as Blake."

Dawkins? Nancy searched her memory, trying to place the name.

"Dawkins was the man on the flight to Los Angeles today?" Nancy asked.

Linda's cheeks whitened. "He was a warning. A way to let me know *Blake* knew I wanted out."

"And when Rod Fullerton wanted out, he was killed," Nancy put in softly.

Linda shuddered.

"What kinds of things does Blake smuggle in?"

"You name it: jewels, art objects, any kind of contraband."

"This Dawkins," Nancy asked, "where does he fit in?"

Once again Linda looked over her shoulder. "Dawkins is Blake's right-hand man. He tampered with Fullerton's brakes, then drove him off the road. He's also a customs agent at Puget Sound Airport."

"A customs agent! Of course!" Nancy said. "That's how the stuff gets through undetected."

"Without Dawkins the whole operation's in jeopardy," Linda said. "He's the key."

"And Sweeney?"

"Sweeney straddles the fence. He's had to do a lot of Blake's dirty work, and I know he'd like to get out, too. But he's like me—he's in too deep." Linda grimaced. "So now what? Are you going to turn me in when we land?"

Nancy thought furiously. "Sean is getting the

police to take care of Maxell. I was so worried about Bess and Jennifer that I just jumped on the plane."

Linda's expression changed. "Why were you worried about Bess and Jennifer?"

Nancy quickly told her what Blake had said. "I got worried, thinking you and Talbot had cooked up something for Bess and Jennifer. At the time I didn't realize it was Maxell, not Talbot, who was the man upstairs."

Linda shook her head emphatically. "I couldn't hurt anyone. I've been a nervous wreck. All I want is a good night's sleep and to be able to look at myself in the mirror again without—"

She broke off suddenly, her eyes widening in horror. Nancy whirled around, expecting to see one of Blake's henchmen bearing down on them. But there was no one in sight. Whatever Linda was seeing was entirely in her own mind.

Linda suddenly reached for Nancy, her hands clutching the folds of her shirt. "He's planning something," she said in a quavering voice. "Blake set this up. Don't you see? He got Jennifer and Bess and me all on this flight and then baited the trap for you, too! He's going to kill us all!" she said on a note of rising hysteria. Then she brushed past Nancy toward the front of the plane.

Nancy took three steps after her, the hair rising on the back of her neck. Blake had set a trap! Linda was right.

"Linda—" Nancy began, heading up the aisle.

Suddenly there was the loudest explosion Nancy had ever heard.

People started screaming. The plane shuddered crazily and dipped sideways. Nancy pitched forward and fell into the aisle, holding on to a seat. Then she heard an ear-splitting wrenching of metal. She glanced back. To her horror she saw the floor at the back of the plane crack open. Before she could take another breath, a gaping hole appeared—and the rear seats started falling out of the plane!

Then the plane went into a steep, spiraling dive. They were going to crash!

Chapter

Seventeen

NANCY CLUNG TO the nearest seat. The inside of the plane grew hazy and bitterly cold. Oxygen masks dropped from compartments above the seats. Passengers shrieked. Magazines and papers blew wildly around and funneled in a tornadolike rush out the hole.

"Remain seated," the pilot's voice said over the intercom. "Put on your oxygen masks. Make certain your seat belts are fastened. Bend over and hold on to your ankles."

Nancy couldn't see a thing. The plane's nose-dive continued. Bess and Jennifer, Nancy thought wildly, please be all right!

She recognized Mark's voice next, calm and

soothing. "We believe a bomb has gone off in the baggage compartment. The dive is so we can equalize pressure and keep the hull from buckling further. Please remain bent down holding on to your ankles. This is for your protection."

Nancy could hear soft sobbing nearby, but the screaming had stopped. Her fingers had gone numb, and her lungs were bursting. She dragged herself to the nearest empty seat and put a mask over her face.

It seemed forever before the plane slowly leveled out. It was still too hazy to see, but Nancy buckled herself in, bent her head down, and grabbed her ankles.

Mark's voice sounded over the intercom again. "We are returning to Puget Sound Airport. The tower has been alerted that we will be making an emergency landing."

Nancy sat tensely. She had seen the hole in the fuselage. She knew how critical their situation was.

Blake Maxell did this! she thought. Risking innocent lives to save his smuggling operation!

When she felt the plane begin to turn, Nancy glanced out the window again. With relief she recognized the tower at Puget Sound Airport.

The plane dropped even lower. But instead of making for the runway, it circled the tower.

They're checking for damage, Nancy thought. Her heart sank. The landing gear might have been damaged in the blast!

Her elbows dug into the armrests as the plane circled several more times. Then it suddenly straightened out and headed for a runway—the runway whose lights Nancy had glimpsed during their turns around the tower.

It was the runway stretching toward the dark waters of Puget Sound. *The northeast runway.*

Mark's words from earlier that day came back to her.

"The northeast runway is five thousand feet long. It's the longest one we've got. When the plane runs out of landing strip, it just keeps heading forward across a field to whatever's in front of it. . . . You'd better hope there's nothing there . . . in a flaps-up landing with no brakes you can imagine what happens. . . ."

Were they going to make a flaps-up landing?

They were approaching the landing strip fast—too fast. Nancy's heart was racing. Her pulse was thundering in her ears. She felt the wheels bump down, and the plane bore forward with tremendous speed.

Instinctively Nancy braced herself for the crash.

The pilot was pumping the brakes; she could feel it. But suddenly the plane surged forward again. Nancy knew what had happened. Hydraulic fluid in the lines to the brakes had been used up.

They were hurtling forward with nothing to stop them!

Then there was a tremendous bump. The plane rattled as if it would actually vibrate apart. Then it slowly came to a halt in the muddy field beyond the runway.

Nancy leapt from her seat. She struggled forward as Linda Cotilla came on the intercom. "Unbuckle your seat belts," Linda ordered. "And come this way."

White and shaking, Bess took her cue from Linda and pulled on the emergency exit over the left wing. Nancy yanked on the red handle over her wing, instantly inflating the rubber slide.

"Jump and slide," Linda was saying over and over again, evacuating the passengers.

Bess and Nancy did the same, hurrying the people out the exits.

"What's that smell?" Bess said suddenly.

Nancy's nostrils quivered. "Smoke!" she answered quietly. "Don't panic. Get everyone out."

They worked as fast as they could. Now every second counted. The bomb had started a fire, and it was spreading rapidly.

The pilot and Mark came out of the cockpit carrying an unconscious Jennifer, whose eyes were just fluttering open.

"Get out," the pilot ordered. "We'll bring Jennifer."

Bess jumped first. Nancy followed. She *whooshed* down the slide and into the arms of waiting firemen who pulled her away from the plane. Then Mark brought Jennifer down, and Linda and the pilot came after them.

Emergency vehicles circled the plane, their

lights whirling. Jennifer was leaning heavily on Mark's arm, but when she saw Nancy, she rushed forward and threw her arms around her friend. "Thank goodness you're all right! What happened?"

"Get back!" one of the firemen suddenly ordered, and Nancy and her friends sprinted for the terminal.

They'd just gotten inside when the plane exploded in a terrific ball of fire.

"Jennifer! Jennifer! Are you all right?"

Sean was running up to meet them. Jennifer threw her arms around him as he hugged her close. "Sean," she whispered.

Nancy hated to interrupt their tender moment, but she had to know about Maxell. "Did you call the police?" she asked Sean.

"You bet I did, and Maxell's in custody. Come on. The police are waiting for us in a private room. They want you to give them a full report."

Later, as dawn was painting lavender streaks of light across the horizon, Preston Talbot walked up to Nancy.

"Are you finished with Ms. Drew yet, Detective Haggarty?" Preston Talbot asked. "I would like to thank her personally on behalf of Victory Airlines."

Nancy yawned and smiled. "Thank you, Mr. Talbot. But I had a little help from my friends, you know."

"I guess we're finished, Ms. Drew," Detective Haggarty said, snapping shut his notebook. "You and your friends can go home and get some sleep."

"Could *I* ask a few questions first?" Nancy asked. "There are some loose ends I'd like to tie up."

"Sure. What do you want to know?"

"I know Blake Maxell planted the bomb on the plane, but how did he do it?"

"It was almost too simple," the detective answered. "He put the bomb in a suitcase and checked it through baggage onto the plane."

"And was it Linda who threw the rock through Preston Talbot's window?" Nancy asked.

"That's right. She was trying to warn you to stay away."

Nancy used this chance to bring up all the reasons she felt Linda should be given special consideration. "I'll see what I can do," Detective Haggarty promised.

"Have you gotten back any of the stolen merchandise?" Nancy finally asked as they wound up the interview.

"Some. The Ming vase Miranda Cummings had in her possession was stolen from her apartment by Grant Sweeney. We recovered that from his apartment—"

"Can I ask something?" Bess spoke up. "How did Maxell know about Nancy? And how did

Linda Cotilla know? We'd barely gotten to Seattle before the rock was thrown through Mr. Talbot's window."

"Good question," Nancy said, turning back to the detective. "I've wondered how they got their information so fast. It kept making me think Mr. Talbot was involved. He was the only one who could know."

Detective Haggarty inclined his head. "I have to hand it to Maxell. He rigged up Talbot's interoffice intercom so it was always on and connected to his own office. That way he could monitor all of the president's conversations. As soon as Jennifer told him you were coming, he was prepared. He warned Linda about you, but—as you know—Linda took the opportunity to warn *you*."

A knock sounded at the door, and another officer strode into the room. "Good news," he said. "Sweeney's been caught, and so has Dawkins. Looks as though this case is just about wrapped up."

"Wow," Bess said sleepily as they walked toward Victory's flight counter a few minutes later. "I can't remember the last time I felt so tired." She leaned against Mark's arm.

"Me, too," Jennifer murmured.

"Uh-oh," Nancy said under her breath when she saw Paul approaching.

"What's wrong?" Bess followed her gaze.

"Hello, beautiful," Paul said, dropping an arm

over Nancy's shoulders. "Maybe we can take up where we left off last night. As I recall, you'd just come around to my way of thinking."

The kiss! Nancy's heart sank. She'd forgotten all about it. "Paul, about that kiss . . ."

"Yeah?"

Feeling everyone's eyes on her, Nancy said helplessly, "It was a diversionary tactic. Done in the line of duty, so to speak."

"Cut the detective mumbo-jumbo. Does that mean we have a date, or not?"

He'd really tried to help. Nancy couldn't bear to let him down. "Tonight, after we've all had some rest, we're going out to celebrate," she said. "We'd love it if you came along."

"I'll be there," Paul said. Then with a grin he added, "You've got great lips, kid."

"Somehow I have the feeling I'm going to regret this," Nancy said.

Mark and Sean kissed Jennifer and Bess goodbye. Nancy looked away and let her thoughts turn to Ned.

After Mark and Sean had left, Jennifer said fervently, "I want you both to know that I'm going to stick to flying! From now on, you can do all the detecting, Nancy. It's too dangerous for me!"

"I'm glad." Nancy stifled another yawn. "And now I think it's time to go home," she said. "I'm done in. What a night!"

"You know, Nancy, I've been thinking," Bess said as they walked to Jennifer's car. "Maybe we should keep the rental car and drive back to River Heights."

"Sorry, Bess," Nancy said. "But we're going to have to fly home. There's someone waiting for me there, and I don't want to waste any more time getting back to him." It was her turn to spend time in the arms of the guy she loved.

Nancy's next case:

Nancy, George, and Ned are off to Montreal, where Nancy's supposed to clear up a small case of corporate blackmail—and maybe get some time off with Ned.

But there's no time for romance when Nancy starts investigating. She's discovered just one string of a monstrous web of blackmail and deceit. And she's found an adversary who seems to know exactly what she'll do—*before* she does it.

Can Nancy win this dangerous game of wits? Find out in *THIS SIDE OF EVIL,* Case #14 in *The Nancy Drew Files*®.

Have you seen
Nancy Drew
lately?

Nancy Drew has become a girl of the 80s! There is hardly a girl from seven to seventeen who doesn't know her name. Now you can continue to enjoy Nancy Drew in a new series, written for older readers – THE NANCY DREW FILES. Each book has more romance, fashion, mystery and adventure.

Join Nancy in all these fabulous adventures, available only in Armada.

ARMADA

Nancy Drew
Mystery Stories

Nancy Drew is the best-known and most-loved girl
detective ever. Join her and her best friends, George Fayne
and Bess Marvin, in her many thrilling adventures available
in Armada.

ARMADA

All these books are available at your local bookshop or newsagent, or can be ordered from the publisher. To order direct from the publishers just tick the title you want and fill in the form below:

Name _____

Address _____

_____

Send to: Collins Childrens Cash Sales
PO Box 11
Falmouth
Cornwall
TR10 9EN

Please enclose a cheque or postal order or debit my Visa/ Access –

Credit card no:

Expiry date:

Signature:

– to the value of the cover price plus:

UK: 60p for the first book, 25p for the second book, plus 15p per copy for each additional book ordered to a maximum charge of £1.90.

BFPO: 60p for the first book, 25p for the second book plus 15p per copy for the next 7 books, thereafter 9p per book.

Overseas and Eire: £1.25 for the first book, 75p for the second book. Thereafter 28p per book.

Armada reserve the right to show new retail prices on covers which may differ from those previously advertised in the text or elsewhere.

ARMADA